Alphonse Daudet

Port Tarascon

the last adventures of the illustrious Tartarin, tr. by Henry James

Alphonse Daudet

Port Tarascon
the last adventures of the illustrious Tartarin, tr. by Henry James

ISBN/EAN: 9783337340193

Printed in Europe, USA, Canada, Australia, Japan

Cover: Foto ©Andreas Hilbeck / pixelio.de

More available books at **www.hansebooks.com**

Alphonse Daudet

ALPHONSE DAUDET

PORT TARASCON

The Last Adventures OF THE ILLUSTRIOUS TARTARIN

TRANSLATED

BY HENRY JAMES

ILLUSTRATED

BY ROSSI, MYRBACH, MONTÉGUT, BIELER
AND MONTENARD

NEW YORK
HARPER & BROTHERS, FRANKLIN SQUARE
1891

TRANSLATOR'S PREFACE.

THE three great episodes in the career of Alphonse Daudet's genial and hapless hero form together so vivid a picture and so complete a history, are so full of reciprocal reference and confirmation, that it is scarcely fair to fix our attention on one of them without bearing the others in mind. They have this quality of the great classic trilogies, that each of them gains in interest by being read in the light of the others, so that the whole work becomes, in its way, a high example of artistic consistency. If the reader turn back to *Tartarin of Tarascon*, of which the main subject is the worthy bachelor's passion for the pursuit of imaginary beasts—of course he is incapable of killing a fly—he will see how the author has vivified the conception from the first, putting into it an intensity of life that could only throb on, hilariously, into new exuberances. Those readers to whom Tartarin's earlier adventures have not been definitely revealed—his visit to Algeria in pursuit of the lion of the Atlas, his wonderful appearance in Switzerland, where he qualifies himself, by rare and grotesque achievements, for the presidency of the Alpine Club of Tarascon, an office in regard to which the bilious Costecalde is his competitor—such uninstructed persons had better turn immediately to the first and second parts of the delightful record. They will there acquire a further insight into some of the matters tantalizingly alluded to in *Port Tarascon*—the baobab and the camel, the lion-skins, the poisoned arrows, the alpenstock of honor, the critical hours passed in a damp dungeon in the Chateau de Chillon.

We must praise, moreover, not only the evocation of the sonorous and sociable little figure of Tartarin himself—broad of shoulder and bright of eye, bald of head, short of beard, belted on a comfortable scale for all exploits—but the bright image of the wonderfully human little town which he has made renowned, and in which the charming art of touching up the truth—the poor, bare, shabby facts of things—is represented as flourishing more than anywhere else upon earth. A compendium of all the droll idiosyncrasies of his birthplace, Tartarin makes them epic and world-famous, hands them down to a warm immortality of condonation. Daudet has humorously described in a "definitive" preface (just as he alludes to them in the opening pages of *Port Tarascon*) some of the consequences, personal to himself, of this accident of his having happened to point his moral as well as adorn his tale with the little patch of Provence that sits opposite to Beaucaire by the Rhone. Guided in his irrepressible satiric play by his haunting sense of the French "Midi," his own provoking, engaging clime, it was quite at hazard that in his quest of the characteristic he put his hand on Tarascon. What he wanted was some little Southern community that he could place in comic and pathetic, at times almost in tragic, opposition to the colder, grayer Northern stripe in the national temperament. Tarascon resented at first such compromising patronage. She shook her plump brown shoulders and tried to wriggle out of custody. The quarrel, however, has now been more than made up, for the sensitive city, weighing the shame against the glory, has not, in the long-run, been perverse enough to pretend that the affair has cost her too much. It was, in fact, in regard to sweet old dusty Roman Nîmes, his native town, that he had permitted himself, in intention, the worst of his irreverences. At any rate, what most readers will say is that if the Tarascon of fact is not like the Tarascon of art, so much the worse for the former.

It is impossible not to ask one's self whether the author foresaw from the first the sequel and the conclusion of Tartarin's life; whether the first episode was a part of a conscious plan. The reason of this curiosity is that everything fits and corresponds so beautifully with everything else—the later developments are contained so in germ in the earlier. But curiosity as to the way exquisite things are produced in literature is an attitude as to which the profit is mainly in the healthy exercise of the faculty; for the questions it presses most eagerly are the most unanswerable. They are not, at any rate, the questions the man of genius himself most confidently meets. It is probable that Tartarin's full possibilities glimmered before his biographer even in the early chapters, but that they remained vague, in their vividness, till they were attempted—just as the lair of the lion and the land of the glacier both attracted and eluded the prudent Tartarin himself, till the rising growl of public opinion put him really on his mettle. The rest of the whole work—its general harmony and roundness—is neatness and tact of execution.

Tartarin's word about himself, quoted from his historian, that he is Don Quixote in the skin of Sancho Panza, is the best summary of his contradictions. The author's treatment of these contradictions is of the happiest; he keeps the threads of the tangle so distinct, and with so light a hand. Whenever life is caught in the fact with this sort of art, what shines out even more than the freshness of the particular case is its general correspondence with our experience. It becomes typical and suggestive and confirmatory in all sorts of ways, and that is how it becomes supremely interesting. The fat little boastful bachelor by the Rhone-side, with his poisoned arrows and his baobab, his perfect candor and his tremendous lies, his good intentions and his perpetual mistakes, presents to us a kind of eternal, essential ambiguity, an antagonism which many fallible souls spend their time trying to simplify. What is this ambiguity but the opposition of the idea and the application—the beauty one would like to compass in life and the innumerable snippets by which that beauty is abbreviated in the business of fitting it to our personal measure? There are two men in Tartarin, and there are two men in all of us; only, of course, to make a fine case, M. Daudet has zigzagged the line of their respective oddities. As he says so amusingly in *Tartarin of Tarascon*, in his comparison of the very different promptings of these inner voices, when the Don Quixote sounds the appeal, "Cover yourself with glory!" the Sancho Panza murmurs the qualification, "Cover yourself with flannel!" The glory is everything the imagination regales itself with as a luxury of reputation—the *regardelle* so prettily described in the last pages of *Port Tarascon;* the flannel is everything that life demands as a tribute to reality—a gage of self-preservation. The glory reduced to a tangible texture too often turns out to be mere prudent underclothing.

Tarascon was inordinately fond of glory. It was this love of glory at bottom that dragged it across the seas, where it so speedily became conscious of a greater need for flannel than its individual resources could supply. Delightful was M. Daudet's idea of illustrating the grotesque and inevitable compromise by the life of a whole community. We have had them all before; they all peep out in the first book of the series — Bézuquet and Pascalon, Bompard and Bravida, Costecalde and Escourbaniès, Mademoiselle Tournatoire and her brother, the blood-letting doctor. We have listened to the mingled nasality and sonority of their chatter, and admired in several cases the bold brush of their mustaches. We move in the aroma of garlic that constitutes their social atmosphere, and that suffuses somehow with incongruous picturesqueness the Gallo-Roman mementos of their civic past. We have already, in *Tartarin of Tarascon*, seen poor Mademoiselle Tournatoire, at her casement, with a face like a white horse, fixing fond eyes, as he passes, on her heroic fellow-townsman. We have heard the shrill of the cicadas on the "Walk Round," and the pipe of the little bootblacks before Tartarin's little gate. We know everything possible about the great man, down to the details of his personal habits and the peculiarities of his pronunciation, and how he knotted his bandanna before he went to bed, and where he kept the poisoned arrows, and where he could put his hand upon Captain Cook, and where upon Bougainville. We have lived with him so intimately that it makes a great difference to us that he has at last played his part out.

The only defect of *Port Tarascon* is that it leaves no more to come; it exhausts the possibilities. But the idea is vivid in it to the end, and poetic justice is vindicated. If the drama is over, it is the drama of the contending spirits. From the moment one of these spirits wins the victory and destroys the equilibrium, there is nothing left for Tartarin but to retire to Beaucaire, and Beaucaire, of course, is extinction. When the Sancho Panza sees his romantic counterpart laid utterly low—I needn't mention where the victory lies, nor take the edge from the reader's own perception of the catastrophe; it is enough to say that the thrill of battle could only be over from the moment such abundant and discouraging evidence was produced of the quantity of compromise it takes to transmute our dreams into action, our inspiration into works—even Sancho Panza, for all his escape, his gain of security, weeps for the prostrate hidalgo. Tartarin is betrayed by his compromises; they rise up and jeer at him and denounce him. But he granted them in good faith; he was unconscious of them at the time. Indeed, he would have perished without them only less promptly than he perishes with them; they were as necessary to save him for an hour as they were predestined to lose him forever.

For all this, it can hardly be said that a book dissuades, however humorously and paradoxically, from action, from the deed to be done, when it is itself a performance so accomplished, so light and bright and irresistible, as the three chronicles of Tartarin. Therefore the last moral of all is, that however many traps life may lay for us, tolerably firm ground, at any rate, is to be found in perfect art.

HENRY JAMES.

INTRODUCTION.

It was September, and it was Provence, when the vintage was coming home, five or six years ago.

From the high wagonette, drawn by the rough horses of the Camargue, that carried us at full speed—Mistral the poet, my son, and myself—towards the Tarascon station and the fast train to Lyons and Paris, the closing day struck us as divine, as it burned itself pale; a day suffused, exhausted, and fevered; passionate, like the fine faces of some women there. There was not a breath of air, in spite of our rattling pace. The rank rushes, with their long ribbony leaves, were straight and stiff by the wayside; and on all the country roads, snowy white with the white of dreams, where the motionless dust creaked beneath the wheels, passed a slow procession of wagons laden with the black grape, nothing but the black, followed by young men and girls, all tall and well set up, long-legged and dark-eyed. Clusters of black eyes and of black grapes; you could see nothing else in the tubs and hods, under the slouched felt hats of the vintagers, and the head-cloth, of which the women kept the corners tight in their teeth. Here and there, in the angle of a field, against the white of the sky, rose a cross with a heavy bunch suspended as a votive offering to each of its arms. "*Ve*—look!" dropped from Mistral, touched and showing it, yet smiling with almost maternal pride in the candid paganism of his people; after which he took up his tale again—some scented, golden story of the Rhone-side, such as the Goethe of Provence sows broadcast from those ever-open hands of his, of which one is poetry and the other reality.

Oh, miracle of words, magic concord of the hour, the scenery, and the brave rustic legend that the poet reeled off for us all along the narrow way, between the fields of mulberry and olive and vine! How well we felt, and how fair and light was life! All of a sudden my eyes were darkened, my heart was compressed with anguish. "Father, how pale you are!" said my son; and I had scarcely strength to murmur,

as I showed him the castle of King René, whose four towers in the level distance watched me come, "There's Tarascon!"

You see, we had a terrible account to settle, the Tarasconians and I! Clever people as they are—like all our people there—I knew their backs were up; they bore me a black grudge for my jokes about their town and about their great man, the illustrious, the delicious Tartarin. I had often been warned by letter, by anonymous threats: "If ever you come through Tarascon, look out!" Others had brandished over me the vengeance of the hero: "Tremble; the old lion has still his beak and claws!" A lion with a beak—the deuce!

Graver still, I had it from a commandant of the mounted police of the region that a bagman from Paris, who, through a sorry identity of name, or simply as a "lark," had signed "Alphonse Daudet" on the register of the inn, had found himself assailed at the door of a café, and threatened with a bath in the Rhone. Our honest Tarasconians have in their blood this game of the ducking.

"Willy-nilly, they shall take the jump from the big window of Tarascon into the Rhone," is the sense of an old Provençal catch of '93, which is still sung there, emphasized with grewsome comments on the drama of which King René's towers were at that time witness. So, as it was not quite to my taste to take a header from the big window, I had always in my journeys south given a wide berth to the good city. And now, this time, an evil fate, the desire to go and put my arm about my dear Mistral, the impossibility of catching the express at another point, threw me straight into the jaws of the beaked lion.

I might have managed it if there had been only Tartarin. An encounter of man to man, a duel with poisoned arrows, under the trees of the "Walk Round"—the public promenade that encircles the place—was

not the sort of thing to frighten me. But the wrath of a whole people—and then the Rhone, the terrible Rhone! Ah, I can tell you, he didn't take up much room at that moment—the author of the two *Tartarins.* In vain Mistral tried to reassure me. "Oh, come! don't mind!

I'll talk to the crowd;" while my boy, a young medical student of the Paris hospitals, took his bistoury out of his instrument case, and prepared resolutely to rip something up. All this only deepened my gloom.

It was a strange thing, but perceptibly, as we drew nearer to the city, there were fewer and fewer people on the ways, and we met fewer of the vintagers' carts. Soon we had nothing before us but the white, dusty road, and all around us, in the country, the space and solitude of the desert.

"It's very queer," said Mistral, under his breath, rather uneasy. "You'd say it was a Sunday."

"If it were a Sunday you'd hear the bells," added my son, in the same tone; for there was something oppressive in the silence that lay upon city and suburb. There was nothing, not a bell, not a cry, not even the jingle of a country cart, clear in the resonant air; yet the first houses of the outer town stood up at the end of the road—one of the oil-mills, the customhouse, newly whitewashed.

We were getting in. And hardly had we advanced into the long street when our stupor was great to find it deserted, with doors and windows closed, without a dog or a cat, a chick or a child—without a creature: the smoky portal of the blacksmith disfeatured of the two wheels that it usually wore on either flank; and the tall trellis-screen, with which the local doorway protects itself against flies, taken in, departed, like the flies themselves, like the exquisite puff of garlic which, at that hour, should have proceeded from the local kitchen.

Tarascon without the smell of garlic! Is that the sort of thing you can fancy?

Mistral and I exchanged looks of awe, and really it was not for nothing. To expect the howl of a delirious people, and to find the place a Pompeii — as silent as death! Farther on, where we could put a name on every dwelling, on all the shops familiar to our eyes from childhood, this impression of the empty and the forsaken was still more startling.

Closed was Bézuquet, the druggist, on the bit of a Square; closed likewise was Costecalde, the armorer, and Rébuffat, the pastry-cook, "the famous place for caramels." Vanished the scutcheon of Notary Cambalalette, and the sign, on painted cloth, of Marie Joseph Escourbaniès, manufacturer of the Arles sausage; for the Arles sausage has always been turned out at Tarascon. I point out in passing this great denial of historic justice.

But, in fine, what had become of the Tarasconians?

Now our wagonette rolled over the Long Walk, in the tepid shade, where the plane-trees interspaced their smooth white trunks, and where never a cicada was singing: the cicadas had flown away! Before the house of our Tartarin, all of whose shutters were closed — it was as blind and dumb as its neighbors—against the low wall of the bit of a garden, never a blacking-box, never a little shoeblack to call out, "A shine, Mossoo?"

"Perhaps there's cholera," one of us said.

At Tarascon, sure enough, on the arrival of an epidemic the inhabitant moves out and encamps under canvas, at a goodish distance from the town, until the bad air has passed by. At this word cholera, which throws every Provençal into a blue "funk," our coachman applied the whip to his steeds, and a few minutes later we pulled up at the steps of the station, perched on the very top of the great viaduct which skirts and commands the city.

Here we found life again, and human voices and faces. The trains were up and down, in and out, on the net-work of rails; they drew up with the slamming of doors, the bawling of stations: "Tarascon; stop five minutes; change

for Nîmes, Montpellier, Cette." Mistral went straight off to the superintendent, an old servant who has never left his platform for five-and-thirty years.

"Well, now, Master Picard, what's the matter? Your Tarasconians—where are they? What have you done with them?"

To which the other, greatly surprised at our surprise: "Where are they? You don't know?

Don't you read anything, then? Yet they've advertised it enough, their island, their Port Tarascon. Well, yes, then, my dear fellow, they've gone, the Tarasconians; gone to plant a colony; Tartarin the illustrious at their head, carrying off with them the symbol of the city—the very Tarasque."

He broke off to give orders, to bustle along the line, while at our feet, erect in the sunset, we saw the towers, the belfries and bells, of the forsaken city, its old ramparts gilded by the sun to the superb tone of a "browned" pasty, and giving exactly the idea of a woodcock pie of which the crust only was left.

"And tell me, Monsieur Picard," asked Mistral of the superintendent, who had come back to us with his good smile—no more uneasy than that at the thought of Tarascon "on the go"—"was this emigration *en masse* some time ago?"

"Six months."

"And you've had no news of them?"

"None whatever."

Cracky! as they say down there. Some time later we had news indeed, detailed and precise, sufficiently so to enable me to relate to you the exodus of this gallant little people under the lead of its hero, and the dreadful misadventures that fell upon it. Pascal has said, "We need the agreeable and the real; but this agreeable should itself be taken from the true." I have tried to conform to his doctrine. My story is taken from the true—put together from letters of the emigrants, from the *Memorial* of the young secretary of Tartarin, and from depositions published in the authorized law reports—so that when you come across some Tarasconade more extravagant than usual, I'll be hanged if I invented it!

BOOK FIRST.

I.

"Franquebalme, old fellow, I'm not happy about France. Our rulers are putting us through."

Uttered one evening by Tartarin before the fireplace of the club, with the gesture and accent that you may imagine, these memorable words are a compendium of what was thought and said at Tarascon-on-the-Rhone two or three months before the exodus. The Tarasconian in general pays little attention to politics; indolent by nature, indifferent to everything that is not a "local interest," he holds for "the state of things," as he calls it. All the same, for some time past there had been a lot of things to be said about the state of things.

"Our rulers are putting us through — the whole thing!" said Tartarin.

In this "whole thing" there was first of all the prohibition of the bull-baiting.

I dare say you know the history of the Tarasconian, a very bad Christian and a reprobate of the worst kind, who, having got into Paradise by stealing a march on St. Peter when his back was turned, refused to go out again, in spite of the supplications of the saintly turnkey. What, in this case, did the great St. Peter do? He sent a whole flock of angels to clamor close to the highest sky, with as many voices as possible: "There! there! the cattle! There! there! the cattle!" which is the call for the great game. Hearkening to this, the ruffian changes countenance.

"You go in for bull-baiting up here, then, great St. Peter?"

"Bull-baiting? Rather! And a splendid kind, old man."

"Where do you have it, then? Where does it take place?"

"Just outside there, in front of Paradise, where there's room to turn round, you know."

At this the Tarasconian rushes out to see,

and the gates of heaven are closed upon him forever.

If I recall this legend, as old as the benches on the "Walk Round," it is to show you the passion of the Tarasconians for the said bull-baiting, and the indignation created by the suppression of their cherished sport.

After this came the order to turn out the White Fathers and close their pretty convent of Pampérigouste, perched on a little hill all gray and fragrant with thyme and lavender—it has been established there for ages—so that from the gates of the town you may see its belfries between the pines.

The Tarasconians were very fond of their White Fathers, so gentle and good and harmless, who had the secret for making an excellent elixir of the fragrant herbs with which the bit of a mountain is covered. They were also famous for their swallow tarts and their delicious *pains-poires*, or potted pears, which are quinces done up in a fine golden paste—whence the name of Pampérigouste given to the abbey. Every Tarasconian used to hear the chimes of the monastery: the odorous breeze brought them in at the dawn with the song of the lark, and in the twilight with the melancholy cry of the curlew.

When the official notification that they were to leave their convent was served on the Fathers, they refused to go; they shut themselves up, determined to stay.

The gentlemen and ladies of Tarascon, you may well believe, took up a stand for their monks—the ladies, and all their sex, in particular, for they are very hot for religion. Urged on by their wives, from fifteen hundred to two thousand of the common sort—dock porters, stevedores on the Rhone boats, those whom the genteel people call the Rabblebabble,* and always send in first to try the water—came and shut themselves up with the Fathers in the pretty convent of Pampérigouste. The good society, the gentlemen of the club, Tartarin at their head, had it also at heart to uphold the holy cause. There was not a minute of hesitation. But people don't throw themselves into such an enterprise without preparation of any kind. That sort of slapdash is only for the Rabblebabble.

Before everything it was a question of costume. So the costumes were ordered, superb habiliments of Crusaders, long black wrappers, with a great white cross on the chest, and

---

* Rafataille.

everywhere else—before, behind, on the shoulders—intertwinings of thigh-bones in braid. It took a long time, in particular, to put on the braid.

When everything was ready the

convent was already invested; the troops surrounded it with a triple ring, encamped in the fields and on the stony sides of the little hill.

The red trousers, in the thyme and lavender,

looked at a distance like a flowering of poppies. You met on the roads continual patrols of cavalry—the carbine on the thigh, the scabbard swinging on the horse's flank, the revolver case in the belt.

But this exhibition of brute force was not the sort of thing to check the intrepid Tartarin, who had resolved to get through at the head of a handful of the gentlemen of the club. In Indian file, flat on their stomachs, ramping on hands and knees, with all the precautions and stratagems of the savages of Fenimore Cooper, they succeeded in wriggling through the lines, in slipping between the patrols, grazing the rows of sleeping tents, and circumventing the sentinels, while they warned each other of dangerous places by an imperfect imitation of the cry of a bird.

Oh, courage was wanted to try such a business on clear nights, when you see as well as by day! It's true that it was quite in the interest of the besiegers to let as many people as possible get into the blockaded precincts. What was wanted was rather to starve the convent out than to carry it by force. Accordingly, the soldiers were ready to look a different way when they saw these prowling phantoms by moonlight and starlight. More than one officer who had taken absinthe at the club with Tartarin recognized him at a distance, in spite of his crusading disguise, and greeted him with a familiar gesture. Once in the place, Tartarin organized the defence. This devil of a fellow had a natural insight into every profession. He had read all the books on all known sieges. He formed his Tarasconians into brigades of militia, commanded by the bold Bravida, and above

all, full of memories of Sebastopol and Plevna, he made them throw up earth, lots of earth, surrounding the devoted edifice with embankments, ditches, fortifications of every kind, whose circle narrowed itself little by little, so that the besieged could scarcely breathe, and were immured behind their defensive works—which was just the thing for the besiegers.

The Tarasconians were none the less delighted with the turn things were taking. They were a wonder to themselves, and their works were a wonder; they talked of nothing but the glacis, the scarp, and the counterscarp, were full of ardor and confidence, and above all, proud of their chiefs—proud of the bold Bravida, major-general of the place, and particularly of their great man of war, their illustrious Tartarin, general-in-chief of the intrenched camp, who knew all about organizing the defence.

Transmuted into a fortress, the convent was subjected to military discipline. So it must always be when the state of siege is declared. Everything was done by beat of drum and blast of bugle. At the faintest early dawn—for the reveille—for a quarter of an hour the tattoo boomed out in the courts, in the corridors, and under the arches of the cloister. They trumpeted also from morning till night; they sounded for prayers, tara-ta, for the treasurer, tara-ta-ta, for the Father Steward, tara-ta-ta-ta, rending the air with short, sonorous, imperious blasts. They bugled for the Angelus, for Matins and Complines. It was a thing to abash the besieging army, which, all abroad in the open air, made far less noise. Over against it, on the top of the little hill, behind the bastions, the piping and strumming, mixed with the tinkle of the chimes, produced the bravest music, and scattered to the four winds a sort of promise of victory, of glad anthem, half warlike and half holy.

The bother was that the besiegers, quite quiet in their lines, without taking the least trouble, victualled themselves easily, and held high revel all day. The land of Provence is a land of delights, and produces all sorts of good things. Clear golden wines, meat-balls, and sausages of Arles, exquisite melons, delicious fruits, special sweets from Montélimar — everything was for the Government troops, and neither crumb nor drop made its way into the blockaded abbey. Accordingly, on one side, the soldiers, who had never been on such a spree, put on flesh so that you could see it grow, and that their tunics were almost bursting. Simply to look at their fine condition, and the plump, shining haunches of their horses, made one admire the nursing plenty of that blessed corner of earth. On the other side, lackaday! the poor Tarasconians, especially the Rabblebabble, rising early, turning in late, overdone, incessantly on the jump, digging and barrowing earth night and day, by the light of the sun and the light of torches, dried up and grew lean till 'twas a pity.

The monks saw with terror that their provisions were giving out. There would soon be no more swallow tarts: such a lot as they had got rid of since the beginning of the siege! The potted pears were coming to an end. Should they be able to hold out much longer? Every day this question was discussed on the ramparts, scorched and cracked by the drought.

"And the cowards don't attack us," said those of Tarascon, shaking their fists at the red trousers that wallowed in the grass in the shadow of the pines.

But the idea of attacking themselves never occurred to them, so strongly has this brave little race the sentiment of preservation.

Only once Escourbaniès, an extremist, spoke of trying a universal sally, with the monks in front, to turn the mercenaries head over heels.

Tartarin shrugged his broad shoulders and answered with a single word: "Infant!"

Then taking by the arm the boiling Escourbaniès, he drew him to the top of the counterscarp, and showing him with a large gesture the cordons of troops drawn up on the hill, the sentinels placed in all the paths:

"Yes or no, are we the besieged? Well, then!"

What was there to say to that? A murmur of approbation rose around him.

"Evidently he's right. It is for them to begin, since they're the besiegers."

So it was seen once more that no one understood the laws of war like Tartarin.

Nevertheless, something had to be settled.

One day the council assembled in the great chapter-house, lighted from high casements, surrounded by sculptured wood-work, and the Father Steward read his report on the resources of the place. All the White Fathers listened, silent, straight upon their "mercies"—a kind of hypocritical half-seat, which allowed them to be seated, though appearing to stand. It was lamentable, the Father Steward's report. What the Tarasconians had made away with since the beginning of the siege! Swallow tarts, so many hundred; potted pears, so many thousand; and so many of this and so many of that. Of all the things he enumerated, with which they had been so well provided at the beginning, there remained so little, so little, that you might as well call it nothing.

Their Reverences were in consternation. They looked at each other with long faces, and agreed that with all these reserves, given the attitude of the enemy, who had no wish to go to the extreme, they might have held out for years without wanting for anything, if only they had been helped. The Father Steward, in a monotonous, dismal voice, continued to read. All of a sudden an uproar breaks in upon him. The door of the hall bursts open. Tartarin appears, a Tartarin excited and tragic, his cheeks flushed, his beard bristling over the white cross of his dress. He salutes with his

sword the Prior, erect upon his "mercy," then the Fathers, and gravely:

"Monsieur le Prieur, I can no longer hold

my men; they are dying of hunger; all the cisterns are empty. The moment has come to surrender the place or to bury ourselves in its ruins!"

What he did not say, but what had, all the same, quite its importance, was that for a fortnight he had gone without his morning chocolate. He saw it in his dreams, rich, smoking, oily, accompanied with a glass of fresh water as clear as crystal. Whereas at present he had come down to the brackish water of the cisterns!

Immediately the council was on its feet, and, in a hubbub of voices all talking at once, expressed a unanimous opinion: "Surrender the place! The place must be surrendered! We must not bury ourselves!" Brother Bataillet alone—he was always excessive—proposed to blow up the convent with the powder that was left. He even offered to fire it himself. But they refused to listen to him, and when night had come, leaving the keys in the doors, monks and militia, followed by Escourbaniès, by Bravida, and by Tartarin, with his handful of gentlemen of the club, in short, the whole garrison of Pampérigouste, filed out of the convent, this time without drum or fife, and wound silently down the hill. It was a fantastic procession in the moonlight. The enemy's pickets let all these good people come out as peacefully as they had let them go in.

This memorable defence of the abbey did the greatest honor to Tartarin: from that day he was the illustrious vanquished of Pampérigouste. But the occupation of their White Fathers' house by the troops left a dark rancor in the hearts of the Tarasconians.

II.

Some time after the dispersal of the monks, Bézuquet, the druggist, was one evening enjoying the cool, the "good of the air," as they say down there, on the bit of a Square, with his pupil Pascalon and the reverend Brother Bataillet. I must tell you that after the closing of the convent the exiled monks had been gathered in by the Tarasconian families. Each of them had wanted his White Father; the people of means, the shopkeepers, the respectable middle class, all had their own; while the poor families clubbed together and went shares in the maintenance of one of the holy men.

You saw a white cowl in all the shops—in that of Costecalde, the armorer, in the midst of the guns, the rifles, and the hunting knives, or beside the counter of Beaumevieille, the haberdasher, behind the rows of silk bobbins—everywhere, in short, reared itself the same figure of a great white bird, a sort of familiar pelican. And the presence of the Fathers was a true blessing in the houses. Gentle, genial, well-bred, discreet, they were never in the way, never took up too much room at the hearth, and yet they maintained there an unaccustomed goodness and sweetness and propriety.

It was as if the people had always had the Holy Spirit in their midst. The men forbore to swear or to say anything the least broad; the women told no more fibs, or very few, and the little ones sat up straight and quiet on their high-chairs.

In the morning, in the evening, at prayer-time, at the meals, for the *Benedicite* and for "grace," the great white sleeves expanded like wings over the assembled family; and with this perpetual blessing on their heads, the Tarasconians could do no less than live in holiness and virtue.

Every one was proud of his own reverend man, and bragged about him and showed him off. Bézuquet's drug shop had had the good fortune to be chosen as a refuge by Brother Bataillet.

He was all nerves, this Brother Bataillet, all

enthusiasm and ardor, genuinely endowed with the eloquence that pleases the people, and renowned for his manner of producing parables and old tales. He was a superb monk—tall, well set up, with a tanned skin and eyes of fire, the head of a Spanish guerilla. Under the long folds of his thick frieze he had really a fine presence, though one of his shoulders was slightly higher than the other, and he walked not quite straight. But no one noticed these trifling defects when he came down from the pulpit after his sermon and cleaved the crowd with his great nose in the air, in a hurry to get back to the vestry, and still quivering and shaken with his own eloquence. The enthusiastic women, as he passed, cut off with their scissors morsels of his white cloak; he was called on this account the "scalloped" Father, and his gown was so soon beyond all use that the convent had great trouble to keep him supplied.

Well, then, Bézuquet was in front of his shop with Pascalon, and opposite to them was Brother Bataillet, sitting astride of his chair. They were so comfortable there, in the serenity of the blessed, that it was a pleasure to breathe; for at that hour for Bézuquet no customer is a customer; it is the same as at night—the poor sick may wriggle as they like—nothing will induce the honest apothecary to put himself out. It is not the hour. He was listening, and Pascalon too, to one of those beautiful stories that his Reverence knew how to tell, while afar, in the town, in the closing hum of a fine summer's day, the band of the garrison sounded the recall.

All of a sudden the pupil sprang up, red and excited, and without considering that he was interrupting his Reverence, cried out, pointing his finger to the other end of the bit of a Square, and stammering according to his wont, "There comes Monsieur Tar-tar-tarin."

We already know what a peculiar personal admiration Pascalon entertained for the great man of Tarascon.

Sure enough, in the sunset, at some distance, Tartarin's well-known form was outlined.

He was not alone, for near him moved a personage in pearl-gray gloves and thoroughly careful attire, who talked with him as they stopped in the Square. Rather, perhaps, it was Tartarin who talked, full of animation and gesticulating for two, while his companion listened, silent, stiff, motionless, perfectly calm.

He was a man of the North, as you could easily see. You know a man of the North in the South by his quiet attitude and the brevity of his slow speech; just as surely as you recognize a man of the South in the North by his exuberance of gesture and of phrase.

The Tarasconians were in the habit of seeing Tartarin often in company with strangers, for nobody ever passed through the town without

stopping to visit, as one of its curiosities, the famous lion-killer, the illustrious Alpine climber, the modern Vauban, for whom the siege of Pampérigouste has created a fresh renown.

From this affluence of visitors had arisen for the whole town an era of prosperity formerly unknown.

The innkeepers made their fortunes, and yet were not the only gainers, for the whole trade of the place was the better; lives of the great man were sold by the booksellers, and you saw nothing in the shop-fronts but his portrait as a climber, as a Crusader, in every possible form, and in every phase of his heroic existence. But this time it was not an ordinary visitor, a chance tourist passing through, who accompanied Tartarin. It was a stranger of mark, as you might see from his grand air and the respectful manner in which the other spoke to him.

They had crossed the Square and had come nearer. Tartarin, with a fine flourish, indicated his companion.

"My dear Bézuquet and your Reverence, let me present you to M. le Duc de Mons."

A duke!—goodness gracious! There had never been one at Tarascon. A camel had been seen there, a baobab,* a lion-skin, a collection of poisoned arrows and of alpenstocks of honor; but a duke, never in the world! Bézuquet had risen; he bowed, rather embarrassed all the same at finding himself, without having

* Tartarin's extraordinary plant, commemorated in the former histories of his life.

been notified in advance, in the presence of so great a personage. He panted:

"Monsieur le Duc—Monsieur le Duc—"

Tartarin interrupted. "Let us go in, gentlemen. We have to talk of grave matters."

He passed first, rounding his back with a mysterious air, and they went into the little consulting-room of the pharmacy, whose glass front, looking out on the Square, served as a show-case for jars of embryos, preserved tape-worms, and little bundles of camphor cigarettes.

The door closed upon them as if they had been conspirators. Pascalon remained alone in the shop. Bézuquet, before disappearing, had told him what to say to any one who should call, and not to allow such people, under any pretext, to come near the consulting-room. The pupil, greatly mystified, began to arrange on the

shelves the boxes of jujube, the bottles of *sirupus gummi*, and other products of the laboratory.

The sound of voices reached him at moments, and he distinguished especially the ringing voice of Tartarin. Then he went nearer the door, trying to catch some snatches of talk. He heard nothing but some strange words: "Polynesia—earthly paradise—sugar-cane—distilleries—free colony." Then an emphatic outbreak from Brother Bataillet: "Bravo! I'm in it." As for the man of the North, confound him! he talked so low—no fire nor flame in *him*—that one heard nothing.

It was no use for Pascalon to flatten his ear against the key-hole. All of a sudden the door burst open, smitten, *manu militari*, by the lusty fist of Brother Bataillet, and the pupil rolled over to the other end of the pharmacy. But the others were so excited that nobody paid attention to the incident.

Tartarin, erect on the threshold, the fire of enthusiasm in his glance, his forefinger lifted to the bundles of poppy-heads drying on the ceiling of the shop, with the gesture of an archangel brandishing the great sword, exclaimed, from the depth of his lungs and with the tone of one inspired:

"God wills it, your Grace. Our work will be great!"

There was a confusion of out-stretched hands seeking each other, mixing with each other, grasping each other, energetic grips intended to seal forever irrevocable pledges. Still glowing with this supreme expansion, Tartarin, erect and taller than ever, quitted the pharmacy with the Duc de Mons.

They continued their circuit of the town, and traversed the bit of a Square, directing their steps towards the residence of Costecalde, the armorer.

Two days later *The Forum* and *The Piper of Tarascon* were full of articles and advertisements on the subject of a colossal enterprise. The heading bore in big letters, "Free Colony of Port Tarascon." Then came stupefying announcements: "For sale, lands at five francs the acre, bringing in several millions of francs a year. Fortune rapid and assured. Colonists wanted."

Exceptional favors were specified for the inhabitants of Tarascon and the country about. Further appeared an historic sketch of the island on which the projected colony was to settle—an island purchased from the King, Nagonko, by the Duc de Mons in the course of his travels. There was also an allusion to certain neighboring islands which might be acquired later, to extend the establishment; but the main insistence was on the principal island—a real promised land, a land of Canaan.

A climate *paradisiacal*, the temperature of Oceanica, very moderate in spite of its proximity to the equator, varying only from one to two degrees, between 25 and 28; the country extremely fertile, extremely wooded and admirably watered, rising rapidly from the sea, which permitted every one to choose the altitude best suited to his temperament. The abundance of springs and watercourses was a guarantee of the establishment on the most reasonable terms of all industries requiring any kind of motive power, and the natural irrigation of the country placed every species of colonial product on a footing, as it were, of exceptional profusion. In fine, provisions abounded, delicious fruits on every tree, game of every kind in the woods and fields, with innumerable fish in the waters. From the point of view of commerce and navigation, a splendid roadstead could contain a whole fleet—a harbor of perfect safety, shut in by breakwaters, with an inner basin and a special one for repairs. Quays, landing-stages, a light-house, a semaphore, steam-cranes—nothing would be wanting.

The work had already been begun by coolies and Australian aborigines, under the direction and on the plans of highly skilled engineers, and of the most distinguished architects. The settlers would find comfortable habitations on their arrival, and even, by ingenious arrangements, with fifty francs more, the houses would be fitted up according to their wants.

You may fancy whether the famous Tarasconian imagination began to work over the perusal of all these wonders. In every family they drew up plans. Every one knocked up a house according to his taste—one dreaming of green shutters, another of a pretty porch; this one having a fancy for brick, and that one for rough stone.

They designed, they tried different things, adding one touch to another—a pigeon-house would be graceful, a weathercock wouldn't look bad.

"Oh, papa, a veranda!"

"Hang it, then; a veranda, my dears!"

For all, it was going to cost! At the same time that these good folk treated themselves so freely to anything they fancied in the way of a pretty cottage, the articles of *The Forum* and *The Piper* were reproduced in all the Southern papers; town and country were deluged with circulars exhibiting little vignettes framed in the palm, the cocoa-nut, the banana, and other outlandish vegetation; the whole province was handed over to a frantic propaganda.

On the dusty roads of the neighborhood Tartarin's gig kept passing at a swinging trot.

Tartarin in person and Brother Bataillet, placed in front, sat as close together as possible, to make a rampart of their bodies for the Duc de Mons, enveloped in a green veil and devoured by mosquitoes, which assailed him with rage on all sides in buzzing battalions, in spite of Tartarin and the Brother, in spite of the veil, in spite of the great whacks his Grace dealt himself. Gorged with the blood of the man of the North, they continued to apply an unrelenting sting to surfaces already completely distended.

For a man of the North was what he was, this fine gentleman! He was never guilty of a gesture, scarcely of a word, much less of an exaggeration. Add to this his coolness—he never got "started," but saw things as they are, and as he himself was. You could feel safe with him, and fear no lies. And then a duke! On the bits of Squares half shadowed with plane-trees and smeared over with great sun spots, in the brown old villages, in the wine-shops eaten up with flies, in the dancing-rooms, and everywhere else, addresses and sermons and lectures went on. The duke, in terms clear and concise, as simple as the naked truth, set forth the delights of Port Tarascon; the eloquence of the monk preached emigration as a crusade; Tartarin, as dusty with his wayfaring as at a battle's close, tossed off a few nervous words, all feeling—words that rolled and swelled —"Victory, conquest, new country." The energy of his gesture seemed to hurl away over every one's head. Or else there were gatherings for discussion, like electoral caucuses, where everything went on by question and answer.

"Are there any venomous animals?"

"Not one. Not a serpent. Not even a mosquito. And in the way of wild beasts, nothing at all."

"But they say that in those parts—far Oceanica—there are anthropophagi."

"Never in the world! They are all vegetarians."

"Is it true that the savages go quite naked?"

"That perhaps may be a little true; but not all; and, at any rate, we'll clothe them."

Articles, advertisements, lectures, everything was wildly successful; the shares were taken up by the hundred and the thousand, the immigrants flowed in, and not only from Tarascon, but from all the South. They came over even from Beaucaire. But there the line had to be drawn. Tarascon thought them very bold, these intruders of Beaucaire. For centuries there has existed between the two towns a rivalry, a muffled animosity, which, fed by innumerable aggravations on one side and the other, by jokes at each other's expense, to say nothing of expressions of contempt, threatens never to die out.

Separated by the whole breadth of the Rhone, the two cities regard each other across the river as irreconcilable enemies. The bridge that has been thrown between them has not brought them any nearer. This bridge is never crossed; in the first place, because it's very dangerous. The people of Beaucaire no more go to Tarascon than those of Tarascon go to Beaucaire.

If you seek to discover the grounds of this inexplicable aversion, they answer you on one side and the other with phrases that explain nothing. "Oh, you know, we know all about them, the Tarascon folk," say the Beaucairenes.

"All the same, we know what they're worth, our neighbors at Beaucaire," say the Tarasconians.

Accordingly, there were to be no Beaucairenes in the settlement of Port Tarascon. First of all, as was quite right, the Tarasconians; afterwards, if any room was left—why, they would see.

But if settlers were not accepted outside of

Tarascon and its cincture, money was accepted from all the world; shareholders were welcome from anywhere and everywhere; the famous acres at five francs (bringing in several thousand francs *per annum*) were disposed of in batches. Accepted too were the gifts in kind which many persons enthusiastic for the work sent in to meet the requirements of the colony. *The Forum* published the lists, and in these lists might have been found the most extraordinary objects.

"A box of little beads.

"A set of numbers of *The Forum*.

"M. Becoulet, forty-five nets, in chenille and beads, for the Indian women.

"Madame Dourladoure, six pocket-handkerchiefs and six knives for the parsonage.

"An embroidered banner for the Orpheon.

"Anduze, of Maquelonne, a stuffed flamingo.

"Six dozen dog-collars.

"A braided jacket.

"A pious lady of Marseilles, a priest's vestment, a trimming for the incense bearer, and a canopy for the pyx.

"A collection of coleoptera under glass."

And regularly, in each list, was mentioned an offering from Mademoiselle Tournatoire: "A complete suit to clothe a savage." Such was the constant preoccupation of this good old maid. All these queer, fantastic contributions, in which the Southern imagination displayed its high, unconscious comicality, made their way by the boxful to the docks, the great receiving houses of the Free and Independent Colony established at Marseilles. The Duc de Mons had fixed there his centre of operations.

From his offices, sumptuously fitted up in splendid apartments, he brewed the business on a great scale, got up companies for distilling from the sugar-cane or for working the "trepang," a species of mollusk of which the Chinese are very fond, and for which, said the prospectus, they will pay any price. Every day, with the indefatigable nobleman, saw the budding of some new idea, the dawn of some great job, which the same evening found quite set on its feet.

In the intervals he organized a committee of shareholders under the chairmanship of the Greek banker Kagaraspaki, and deposited their funds with the Ottoman bankers Pamenyai ben Kaga, an extraordinarily safe house, conspicuous for its prudence in whatever it took up.

Tartarin now passed his life—a feverish life—in travelling from Tarascon to Marseilles, and from Marseilles to Tarascon. He kept the enthusiasm of his fellow-citizens up to the mark, pushed on the local propaganda, and then suddenly dashed off by express to be present at some board, some meeting of stockholders. Every day his admiration for the duke increased.

He, dear fellow, always on the gush, and instinctively mistrustful, perhaps, of himself, held up as an example to every one the duke's coolness and the duke's judgment.

"No danger of exaggeration with him. *He* produces none of those deceptive atmospheric effects that Daudet is fond of charging us with."

On the other hand, the duke showed himself little, and talked even less than in the beginning. The man of the North effaced himself before the man of the South, put him always in the foreground, and left to his inexhaustible loquacity the care of all explanations, of all promises, of all pledges. He contented himself with saying:

"Mr. Tartarin alone knows my whole thought."

And you may judge whether Mr. Tartarin was proud!

III.

One morning Tarascon woke up with this telegram pasted on all the street corners:

"The *Farandole*, a great sailing-ship of twelve hundred tons, has just left Marseilles at dawn, carrying in her bosom, with the fortunes of a whole people, an assortment of goods for the savages, and a cargo of agricultural implements. Eight hundred emigrants on board, all Tarasconians, among whom are Bompard, Provisional Governor of the Colony; Bézuquet, chemist-physician; the Reverend Father Vezole; and Notary Cambalalette, Assessor of Taxes. I myself have seen them out into the open. Everything well. The duke radiant. Print this. TARTARIN OF TARASCON."

This telegram, posted up all over the town by the care of Pascalon, to whom it was addressed, filled the place with jubilation. The streets had put on their holiday look, all the world was out-of-doors, every one wishing to read the blessed despatch; and knots of people stopped before each placard, the words of which were repeated from mouth to mouth: "Eight

hundred emigrants—Tartarin seen them out into the open—the duke radiant." There was not a single Tarasconian who was not as radiant as the duke.

It was the second batch of emigrants that Tartarin, invested by the Duc de Mons with the fine title and the important functions of Governor of the Free and Independent Colony of Port Tarascon, had forwarded in this manner to Marseilles on its way to the

promised land. A month before he had also seen out into the open the first batch, borne off by the steamer *Lucifer*, and this first shipment had been effected under as happy auspices as the second.

The same telegram, the same enthusiasm, the same radiance of the duke. But the *Lucifer*, which had sailed a month ago, had not yet passed the entrance of the Suez Canal. Arrested there by an accident—the breakage of her horizontal shaft—this rather shaky old steamer, a second-hand purchase, had to wait to be helped and rescued by the *Farandole* before she could continue her journey.

This accident, nevertheless, which might have seemed of bad omen, had not in the least chilled, on the part of the Tarasconians, the desire to try their hand at founding a new State. It is true that on this first vessel only the Rabblebabble had been shipped—the people of the commoner sort, you know—those that are always sent on first. The broken shaft, the forced stop, the delay in the voyage, had therefore not had the same importance as if the distressed ship had carried the Tarasconians of mark.

On the *Farandole*, also, there had been a further instalment of the Rabblebabble, accompanied by a few of the wilder spirits, like Notary Cambalalette, Assessor of Taxes of the colony. The good druggist Bézuquet, a man of peace, in spite of his formidable mustaches, fond of his little comforts, afraid of the heat and the cold, little inclined to distant and dangerous adventures, had resisted long before consenting to be despatched.

Under Tartarin's pressure, to all his arguments — "Bézuquet, we owe ourselves to the work; it is for *us* to set the example" — he had at first answered only by dubious head-shakes. It cost him too much to leave the snug shell of his pharmacy and exchange for the pitching and rolling of a cabin his sound naps in the little consulting-room with the tape-worms. To overcome his resistance nothing less had been required than the diploma of a full physician.

Bézuquet had coveted all his life this blessed scroll, which the Governor of Port Tarascon now conferred upon him by private authority.

The Governor, indeed, conferred, by the same authority, many other parchments and patents and commissions, appointing directors, sub-directors, secretaries, commissaries, grandees of the first class and the second class, all of which permitted him to gratify the taste of his compatriots for everything in the way of honors, distinctions, costumes, and braids.

With Father Vezole, who had taken the same ship as Cambalalette and Bézuquet, there had not been the least difficulty. He was such a thorough good soul Father Vezole, always ready for anything and pleased with everything.

saying "God be praised!" to everything that happened: "God be praised!" when he had had to leave the convent; "God be praised!" when they had thrust him on shipboard along with the fortunes of a people, the assortment of goods for the savages and the Rabblebabble, with instructions to say mass on Sundays, to receive the confessions of the emigrants, to attend the last moments of those about to die, and to baptize any little settlers who might come into the world.

As for the members of the nobility and of the upper middle class, before paying with their persons they had paid with their pocket-books, as subscribers, which was very handsome to begin with. For the rest, there was no hurry; while they showed plenty of ardor and faith, they were not sorry to leave those who had preceded them time to send back news of their arrival at Port Tarascon, so that the state of affairs might be fully known.

You may easily conceive that Tartarin, in his quality of Governor, organizer, representative of the idea of the Duc de Mons, was able to leave France only with the last batch. While he waited for the day so impatiently desired, on which he should set foot on the vessel that was to carry him beyond the seas at the head of the best society of Tarascon, he displayed the energy and activity which we have been free to admire in all his undertakings. He seemed to have a fiery flame in his body.

Perpetually on the rush, from Tarascon to Marseilles and from Marseilles to Tarascon, as difficult to catch as a meteor impelled by an invincible force, he appeared in either of these cities only to leave it instantly for the other.

"You are tiring yourself out, mum-mum-master," stammered Pascalon, on the evenings on which the great man came to the pharmacy with a steaming brow and a rounded back.

But Tartarin straightened himself to his height. "I'll rest out there. No, Pascalon, to our work!"

The pupil had been in full charge of the shop ever since Bézuquet's departure, but he superadded to this responsibility functions much more important.

To push on the propaganda so well started, Tartarin had established a journal, *The Port Tarascon Gazette*, and named Pascalon editor-in-chief.

In this character the youth carried on the paper quite alone, from the first to the last line. under the instructions and the superior direction of the Governor.

It is true that this combination was slightly injurious to the interests of the pharmacy: the articles to write, the proofs to correct, the rushing round to the printer's, left the good druggist's representative but little time to occupy himself conscientiously with laboratory work. But the paper before everything!

The *Gazette* treated the public of the metropolis every morning to the latest news of the settlement; it contained articles on its resources, its beauties, its magnificent future, and also published small items, miscellanies, and various kinds of tales.

There was something for every taste.

There were accounts of exploring parties in the islands, conquests, fights against the savages, for bold and adventurous spirits. To the country gentlemen were offered stories of the pursuit of game in the forest, and others, equally astonishing, of that of fish in rivers extraordinarily stocked, together with a description of the methods and the tackle of the natives of the country. Persons of a more peaceful habit —shopkeepers, good sedentary citizens—were delighted to read about some fresh luncheon on the grass, on the edge of a tumbling brook, in the shadow of the great outlandish trees they could fancy they were already there; they could feel the juice of luscious fruits—mangoes, pineapples, and bananas—trickle between their teeth. "And no flies!" said the newspaper; which added a charm the more, flies being, as is well known, the scourge of all picnics and excursions on Tarascon soil.

The *Gazette* even published a novel—"The Maid of Tarascon"—about the daughter of a colonist abducted by the son of a Papuan king who had fallen in love with her; and the ups and downs and ins and outs of this love drama opened boundless horizons to the imagination of young persons.

The financial department was devoted to quotations from the colonial markets, to advertisements of the issue of allotments of land, or of shares in refineries or distilleries, as well as to the publication of subscribers' names and of the lists of contributions in kind, which continued to flow in. The preoccupation of the good lady who wished to clothe a savage kept constantly turning up. It was the dream of her life—perhaps a religious vow.

To meet the demand for such frequent shipments of a complete suit for a savage, she must have set up regular workshops under her roof.

But this innocent spinster was not the only one to become conscious of the fermentation of strange conjectures, thanks to such an explosion of the colonizing spirit, of the idea of expatriation on behalf of countries so far away and so little known.

One day Tartarin had remained quietly at home in his little house, his feet in his slippers and his person snugly enveloped in his dressing-gown; not unoccupied, however, for near him, on the table, were scattered books and papers. He had there at hand the accounts of the explorations of Bougainville and Dumont d'Urville, works on colonization, and hand-books on different kinds of tillage. In the stillness of his study, amid his poisoned arrows, with the shadow of the baobab trembling delicately on the blinds, he "got up" the subject of his settlement and stuffed his memory with information extracted from books. Between whiles he sought relief from these researches in signing some patent, in appointing a Grandee of the first class, or in creating some new public function. And this was not the least arduous part of his task, given the delirious ambition of his fellow-citizens and the impossibility of satisfying them all.

While he was thus occupied, rounding his eyes and blowing into his cheeks, it was announced to him that a lady, dressed in black, veiled, and refusing to give her name, requested to speak to him. She had not even been willing to come in and wait in the garden. Tartarin rushed out to her just as he was -- in his slippers and dressing-gown. The day was drawing to a close, objects were growin already indistinct in the twilight; but in spite of her thick veil, simply by the fire of the two eyes that glowed beneath the tissue, Tartarin recognized his visitor as soon as he was near her.

"Madame Escourbaniès!"

"Monsieur Tartarin, you see before you a most unhappy woman!"

Her voice trembled; it was full of tears. The good fellow was quite moved by it. He took the hand of Madame Escourbaniès and, with a paternal accent:

"My poor Evelina, what's the matter? Tell me!"

Tartarin called almost all the ladies in town by their baptismal names. He had seen them as little girls; as a municipal officer he had been present when they were civilly married; he was their confidant, their friend, almost their uncle.

He had taken Evelina's arm, and they strolled together round the little tank with the gold-fish. Then she told him her trouble, her conjugal anxieties.

From the beginning of the talk about the settlement her husband had tried to worry her. On every pretext he broke out:

"You'll see—you'll see when once we are over there in Polygamilia!"

She, poor thing, very jealous, but also very simple and even a little silly, had taken his teasing quite seriously.

"Is this true, Monsieur Tartarin? Is it true that in that dreadful country men may marry several times?"

He reassured her as best he could. "No, indeed, my dear Evelina; you are quite wrong. All the savages in that quarter are monogamous. Their morals are perfectly correct. Besides, under the direction of our White Fathers, there's nothing to fear in that line."

"And yet the very name of the country—this Polygamilia."

Then only he understood the joke that her great trifler of a husband had tried to make, and he burst into a loud laugh. "He is making fun of you, my dear. The name of the country is not Polygamilia, but Polynesia, which doesn't even sound much like it. It means a great lot of islands."

He went on some time longer, walking her about the little garden, soothing down her jealousy, explaining her husband's bad pun, which at first she had some difficulty in understanding, and comforting her so kindly and completely that she ended by laughing with him over her blunder.

Meanwhile the weeks went by, and still no letters arrived from the actual settlers; nothing arrived but telegrams—telegrams forwarded by the duke from Marseilles. They were very laconic, dashed off hurriedly from Aden, from Sydney, from the different places where the *Farandole* had put in. After all, there was no such great ground for surprise, so notorious and so insurmountable is the indolence of the Tarasconian.

Why should they have written? Telegrams were quite sufficient. Those that were received and regularly published in the *Gazette* brought nothing but good news—a delightful voyage, a sea of oil, every one perfectly well.

Nothing more than this was needed to keep up the general zeal.

At last one day at the very top of the *Gazette*, appeared the following "cable," forwarded like the rest from Marseilles:

"Arrived Port Tarascon.—Triumphal Entry.—Friendship struck up with Natives coming to meet us on Pier.—Tarasconian Flag floats over Town-hall.—*Te Deum* sung in Metropolitan Church.—Everything ready; come quick!"

There came next a dithyrambic article, dictated by Tartarin, on the occupation of the new father-land, the foundation of the young city, the visible protection of God, the flag of civilization planted in virgin soil, the future open to all.

No more was wanted to overcome the very last hesitations. A new issue of shares at a hundred francs an acre was rapidly taken up. The bourgeoisie, the clergy, the nobility—the whole place wished to start instantly; the thing became a monomania, a fever, so that even the grumblers like Costecalde, those who up to this time had been lukewarm and even had affected doubts, were now most crazy to get off.

The preparations were pushed forward on all sides. The nailing of boxes went on in the very streets, littered with straw and hay. The bang of the hammer was heard from morning till night. Men worked in their shirt-sleeves, all in good-humor, singing and whistling, and tools were borrowed and lent from hand to hand, while the liveliest remarks were exchanged. The women packed up their finery, the Fathers their *ciboria*, the little ones their little toys. The vessel chartered for the genteel portion of Tarascon had been christened the *Tootoopumpum*, the popular name of the Tarasconian tambourine, the national musical instrument that presides at the dances and the reels. It was a large iron steamer, commanded by Captain Scrapouchinat, of Toulon, a seaman of wide experience. They were all to go on board at Tarascon itself.

The waters of the Rhone were fair, and as the ship had not a great draught, it had been possible to bring it up the river as far as the town and moor it at the quay. The lading and stowing took a whole month.

While the sailors were arranging the innumerable boxes in the hold, the future passengers settled themselves in advance in their cabins.

And it was a pleasure to see with what jollity, what delightful good-humor, all this went on. Every one was pleased, and only wanted to render service to every one else.

"This place suits you better? Don't mention it!"

"This cabin pleases you more? Make yourself comfortable!"

And so with everything. The Tarasconian

nobility, usually so sniffy, the Aigueboulides, the Escudelles, people who usually looked down at one from the bridge of their great noses, now fraternized with their social inferiors.

In the midst of the hurly-burly of going on board, a letter was received one morning from Father Vezole, dated from Port Tarascon. It was the first mail that had arrived.

"God be praised, we've got here!" said the good Father. "We're in want of a good many little things."

There was not much enthusiasm in this letter, neither were there many details about the colony. The reverend gentleman confined himself to a few remarks about the King, Nagonko, and about Likiriki, the young daughter of the King, a charming little thing whom he had presented with a beaded net for her hair. He requested further that they should send on a few objects slightly more practical than the habitual gifts of the subscribers. This was all. Not a single word about the harbor, about the town, about the settlement. Brother Bataillet was furious.

"He seems to me very slack, your Father Vezole," he said to Tartarin; "but trust me to shake him up for you when I get there."

This letter was indeed very cold, especially coming from such a genial person; but the bad effect that it might have produced was lost in the confusion of getting settled on board, in the deafening noise of the transplantation of a whole city.

The Governor—Tartarin was now called only by this name—passed his days on the deck of the *Tootoopumpum*. With a smile on his face and his hands behind his back, he walked up and down amid a confusion of strange things—bread baskets, chests of drawers, warming-pans—which had not yet found stowage in the hold. He gave advice in a patriarchal tone: "You're taking too many things, my children. You'll find everything you want over there."

Thus he had left behind him his arrows, his baobab, and his goldfish. Of course he was taking his arms—his American rifle, the thirty-two shooter—and also some flannel, plenty of flannel.

And how he looked after everything; how he had an eye on everything, not only on board, but also on shore, from the rehearsals of the Orpheon to the drill of the militia on the Long Walk! This military organization of the Tarasconians had survived the siege of Pampérigouste; it had even been carried further, in view of the defence of the colony, and the conquests that there was a good expectation of making. Tartarin was delighted with the martial attitude of his troops, and frequently expressed his satisfaction to them as well as to their chief, the bold Bravida, in orders of the day.

And yet there was a fold in the Governor's brow.

Two days before they set sail, Barafort, a fisherman on the Rhone, had found among the osiers of the bank an empty bottle, hermetically corked, of which the glass was still clear enough to permit something like a roll of paper to be perceived inside. There's no fisherman who doesn't know that a waif of this kind is to be handed over to the authorities; so Barafort had carried his treasure-trove to the Governor, the only authority now recognized by the Tarasconians. Here, therefore, is the strange letter contained in the mysterious bottle:

"*Tartarin, Tarascon, Europe:*

"Appalling cataclysm at Port Tarascon. Island, city, harbor, swallowed up; sunk out of sight. Bompard admirable as usual, and as usual paying for his devotion with his life. Don't come! In Heaven's name let no one come!"

This letter was evidently the production of a practical joker. How had it ever been carried from the depths of Oceanica and cast ashore precisely at Tarascon? What mighty wave could have floated it so far across the seas? And the "paying as usual with his life," didn't that alone betray a misleading intention? Never mind, this portent disturbed the triumph of our friend.

IV.

You talk of the picturesque, but if you had seen the deck of the *Tootoopumpum* that May morning in 1881 you would have seen something that deserved the name. All the Commissioners and Directors were in full dress. Tournatoire, General Commissioner of Health; Costecalde, General Commissioner of Agriculture; Bravida, General-in-Chief of the Levies, and twenty others, offered to the eye a medley of variegated costumes, blazing with color and embroidered with silver and gold. Many wore in addition the mantle of Grandee of the first class—crimson, trimmed with gold. Amid the bedizened throng Brother Bataillet made a white spot as Grand Almoner of the Colony and Chaplain of the Governor.

The military especially glittered. The greater number of the common soldiers having been forwarded in the other vessels, those that remained were the officers—Bravida, Escourbaniès, the whole staff, sabre in hand, revolver in the belt, the chest well forward, the shoulders well back, in smart hussar jackets, all shoulder-knots and frogs. They were particularly proud of their magnificent boots, polished till they shone again.

With all this military toggery was mingled the finery of the ladies, who were almost all in bright, gay, shimmering colors, with ribbons and scarves that floated in the air. Here and there among the maid-servants was a specimen of the Tarascon head-dress. Hang over all this, in your mind, and over the ship, with its shining brasses, its masts pointed at the sky—hang over this a splendid sun, a real holiday sun; give it for horizon the broad Rhone, billowed like a sea and brushed up by a stroke of our mistral, and you will have an idea of the appearance of the *Tootoopumpum* when about to start for Port Tarascon.

The Duc de Mons was to have been present at the last, but he was in London at this moment, looking after a new issue of bonds. You see, there had been a tremendous need of money to pay for ships and crews and engineers, and to meet the other expenses of the exodus. The duke had announced by telegram that very morning that he was on the point of sending on cash. Every one admired the practical side of the man of the North.

"He goes by book; he looks after the sinews of war," said the Tarasconians, merrily.

"What an example he sets us gentlemen!" Tartarin exclaimed. And he never failed to add, "Now don't get starrted, you know!" rolling his *r* like the good Tarasconian he was. In the midst of the bedizened crowd of his subjects, as they might be called, the Governor remained perfectly simple, only in evening dress, with the grand Ribbon of the Order across his chest.

As each new family arrived to embark it was greeted with acclamations. From the deck of the *Tootoopumpum* they were seen coming down and rounding the corners; and as the groups came nearer and emerged upon the dock they were recognized, they were even addressed by name:

"Ah, here come the Roquetaillades!"

"I say, Monsieur Franquebalme!"

Whereupon there were bravos and enthusiastic cheers. An ovation was made, among others, for the ancient dowager Countess of Aigueboulide, who was almost a hundred years old, as she was seen skipping up the plank in her little black silk mantilla, nodding her head, carrying

in one hand her foot-warmer and in the other her stuffed parrot.

Every moment there were fewer left behind, and soon nobody at all: the streets looked wider now, between the closed doors of the houses, with the shop-fronts all barricaded, and the shutters drawn and blinds lowered on the other windows. When every one was on board there was a period of solemn silence, a deep momentary return of the company on itself. Nothing was heard but the hiss of the escaping steam. Every one had his eyes turned to the captain, erect upon the poop, ready to give the order to let go. All of a sudden somebody cried, "I say, the Tarasque!"

I'm sure you will have heard some mention of this strange creature, the fabled animal that originally gave its name to the city of Tarascon. To recall its history in two words, this Tarasque, in very ancient days, was nothing less than a terrible monster, a most alarming dragon, which laid waste the country at the mouth of the Rhone. St. Martha, who had come into Provence after the death of our Lord, went forth and caught the beast in the deep marshes, and binding its neck with a sky-blue ribbon, brought it into the city captive, tamed by the innocence and piety of the saint.

Ever since then, in remembrance of the great service rendered by the holy Martha, the Tarasconians have kept a holiday, which they celebrate every ten years by a procession through the city. This procession forms the escort of a sort of ferocious, bloody monster, made of wood and painted pasteboard, who is a cross between the serpent and the crocodile, and represents, in gross and ridiculous effigy, the dragon of ancient days. The thing is not a mere masquerade, for the Tarasque is really held in veneration; she is a regular idol, inspiring a sort of superstitious, affectionate fear. She is

called in the country the Old Granny. The creature is usually stalled in a shed especially hired for her by the town council.

So she really formed part of the city, and it was out of the question, on such an occasion, to leave her behind. The start was delayed, and a lot of young men rushed off to fetch her.

When she appeared upon the deck, dragged by these zealous youths, every hat went off and every eye filled. She was greeted with enthusiastic cries; she was the Old Granny indeed, the soul of the city, the Mother-land herself.

Far too big to be stowed away below, she was placed far aft, solidly moored to the deck, and there, enormous and preposterous, like a monster in a pantomime, with her canvas belly and her painted scales, she finished off the quaint picturesqueness of the whole. Rearing her head above the bulwarks, she seemed, like the chimeras carved of old on the prows of ships, to preside over the fortune of the voyage and to subdue the wrath of the sea. She was surrounded with respect; she was occasionally even spoken to; they appeared to invoke her.

Seeing this emotion, Tartarin feared that she might excite in some hearts a regret for the forsaken home; so that, on a sign from him, Captain Scrapouchinat suddenly, in a formidable voice, gave the order, "Straight away!"

This order broke the spell.

Then instantly broke out the flourish of the trumpets and the whistle of the steam; the water began to boil beneath the screw, and amid the hubbub and movement Escourbaniès rushed about, waved his arms, and shouted, "A lot of noise!—let's make a lot of noise!" The shore was left behind at a bound, King René's towers in the distance were more and more reduced, and more and more dwarfed, as if obliterated suddenly by the hot, throbbing light.

Our friends, leaning over the sides of the ship, confident, careless, and smiling, watched all this pass from them and vanish away without more emotion, now that they were accom-

panied by the good Tarasque, than a swarm of bees changing their hive to the sound of the kettle-drum, or a flock of starlings starting in a triangle for Africa.

And truly their beloved monster protected

them. The weather was divine, the sea resplendent, without either gale or gust—never, in short, was there a more auspicious voyage.

At the Suez Canal, indeed, they hung out their tongues a little, toasted at the fire of a burning sun, in spite of the colonial head-gear which all had adopted in imitation of Tartarin—a cork helmet covered with white linen and embellished with a veil of green gauze. But if the temperature was that of an oven, they managed to bear it, having been already tolerably well cooked and prepared for the climate by the sun of Provence. After Port Said and Suez, after Aden and the crossing of the Red Sea, the *Tootoopumpum* took her course straight through the Indian Ocean. She steamed very fast, at a steady pace, on a smooth sea, under a sky as white, as milky, and velvety as one of those wonderful creamy compounds of garlic that the emigrants consumed at every meal.

And oh, the quantity of garlic that *was* consumed on board! They had brought with them a prodigious supply. The odor of it, like a long trail, marked the track of the ship; it seemed as if the very breath of Provence had followed the Tarasque across the waters. As they went on and on, the smell of Tarascon mingled with the smell of India.

Soon they began to skirt the islands that emerged from the deep like clumps of strange flowers. In the midst of the rank verdure flitted magnificent birds, all dressed in gems. The calm, transparent nights, lighted by a myriad

stars, were suffused with vague murmurs—murmurs that might have been the echo of the distant music of bayaderes.

They put in at the Maldives, at Ceylon, at Singapore; but the ladies, Madame Escourbaniès at their head, forbade their husbands to set foot on shore.

A fierce instinct of jealousy caused them to dread this dangerous Indian clime, where love indeed seemed to float in the air. This was felt on the very deck of the *Tootoopumpum*, as you might see in the evening from the way the timid Pascalon leaned against the bulwarks, close to Mademoiselle Clorinde des Espazettes, a tall, handsome girl whose aristocratic charm attracted him.

The good Tartarin smiled in his beard, and looked another way, as soon as he saw these young persons conversing together in the distance with their eyes bent on the sea or turned up to the sky. This spectacle touched him in a tender place; he could see there, in advance, a marriage for their landing.

Besides, from the beginning of the trip, the Governor had shown himself exquisitely kind, charmingly, fondly indulgent, with a particular command of his temper.

Captain Scrapouchinat, who had proved an awkward customer, gloomy and violent, was a regular tyrant on his ship. Unacquainted with laughter, he kept apart from the rest, flew into a rage at the least word, and began to threaten, to talk immediately of having you "shot like

Rosi

Brother Bataillet, his irrepressible chaplain, always ready for rebellion, and always saying to him, "Only make a sign, and I'll chuck him overboard!"

Tartarin took the other's arm, repeated his

"Now don't get started!" and called attention to his own example. Didn't he himself, he the Governor, submit to Scrapouchinat's whims?

He even tried to make excuses for him "The man wants to be master on his own ship After all, he is right."

In this way Tartarin did his best to keep peace on board; but this was not all he did.

The morning hours were devoted to the study of Papuan. It was his chaplain who officiated as teacher; in his character of retired missionary Brother Bataillet knew this language and many others. During the day Tartarin collected his little multitude either on the deck or in the saloon, and gave them lectures, exhibiting his lately learned lore on the subject of the planting of the sugar-cane and the working of the trepang.

But the great wonder was the shooting lessons that he gave the military; for they would find lots of game where they were going. It would not be as at Tarascon, where, for lack of this commodity, the Tarasconians had become, as will be remembered, famous cap-shooters, every one throwing his cap into the air to hit it on the wing.

"You fire very well, my children; but you fire too fast," said Tartarin.

Their blood was too hot; that would never do where they were going.

So he gave them excellent advice, taught them to take their time according to the different kinds of game, and count methodically, as if with a metronome.

"Three times for the quail! One, two, three—bang! Hit! For the partridge"—and fluttering his open hand he imitated the flight of the bird—"for the partridge you must count only two. One, two—bang! Pick her up, she's dead."

So they got through the monotonous hours

of the voyage, and each turn of the screw brought nearer to the realization of their dreams the honest souls who had been cradled all the way in fine projects for the future, sailing in the light of their hopes, and talking of nothing but furnishing, clearing, improving their future estates.

Sunday was always a day of rest and a holiday.

Brother Bataillet said mass on the deck in great pomp, with a full military display; and the bugles rang out and the drums beat the charge at the moment the priest lifted the Host. After mass the reverend Father delivered himself of one of those vivid parables in which he excelled—not so much a sermon as a kind of poetic mystery, all glowing with the Southern faith. The story was as artless as some legend of saints pieced together on the windows of an old village church; but to taste the full charm of it you must imagine the vessel mopped from stem to stern, with all her brasses shining, the ladies seated in a circle, the Governor in his great cane chair, surrounded by the Commissioners in full dress, the troops in two rows, the sailors perched in the shrouds, and the whole congregation silent, attentive, with its eyes upon the Father, who stands erect upon the steps of the altar. The beat of the screw keeps time to his voice, and against the pure deep sky the smoke of the steamer draws out in a straight thin line; the dolphins sport on the surface of the water; the

sea-birds, the gull and the albatross, whirl and cry in the wake of the ship; and the White Father, with his crooked shoulder, himself looks. when he raises and shakes his wide sleeves, like a great sea-bird flapping its wings and about to take flight.

V.

It is again into Paradise that I shall introduce you, my children, into that great antechamber of royal blue where good St. Peter makes his home, his bunch of keys in his belt, ever ready to open his door to the souls of the elect when any present themselves. Unhappily, for years and years past, our humanity has become so wicked that the best of us after death have to stop in purgatory, without going higher, so that the good saint has nothing to do but to rub up his keys with sand-paper, and brush away the cobwebs that are stretched across his door like seals of the law. Every now and then he fancies some one is knocking. Then he says:

"Here's some one at last: it's none too soon."

Then, when the wicket opens, there's nothing but immensity, nothing but eternal silence, with the planets either motionless or rolling through space with the soft sound of a ripe orange detached from the branch; never the shadow of one of the blessed.

Think what a humiliation for a saint so fond of us all, and how he must bewail it day and night! How many he must shed of those burning, consuming tears that have ended by digging down his old cheeks two deep ruts, just like those you may see between Tarascon and Montmajour, on the road to the quarries!

Now, it happened once that St. Joseph, who had come to keep him company a bit—for the poor turnkey was weary at last of being always alone in his forecourt—it happened once that St. Joseph said to him, by way of consolation:

"But, when it comes to that, what difference can it make to you whether or not those people down there continue to come up to your wicket? Aren't you all right here, lulled by the softest music and the sweetest scents?"

Even while he spoke thus there was wafted from the depths of the seven heavens that opened out there, one into another, a warm breeze charged with sounds and colors and perfumes such as nothing, my dear friends, can give you a notion of, not even this flavor of citronade and fresh raspberry which the breath of the sea has been blowing for the last minute into our faces, out of that great bouquet of islands there, pink in the breeze.

"Heigh!" said good St. Peter. "I've more than my share of comfort in this paradise of every blessing, but I wish those poor children could be up here with me." Then, abruptly, seized with anger: "Ah, the scoundrels! Ah, the idiots! No, Joseph. Don't you see the Lord is too kind to such wretches? If I were in His place, I know very well what I should do."

"What would you do, my good Peter?"

"Oh, sure, I'd let fly a great kick at the ant-hill, and send humanity about its business."

St. Joseph jerked up his old beard. "It would have to be terribly strong, all the same, any kick that would demolish the earth. It might do the business for the Turks, the infidels, the populations of Asia that are rotting away; but the Christian world is another matter, solid and strong, put together by the Son."

"Just so," replied St. Peter. "But what Christ has put together Christ can quite as well destroy. I would send my Divine Son down to the gallows-birds a second time, and this Antichrist, who would be my Christ disguised, would make short work of them—reduce them all to pulp."

The good saint spoke in his anger, without heeding much what he said, above all, without suspecting that his words would be repeated to the Divine Master; so that his surprise was great when suddenly the Son of Man rose before him, with a little bundle on his shoulder, at the end of a wayfarer's staff, saying, with his firm, sweet voice,

"Come, Peter; I take you with me."

From the paleness of Jesus, from the fever of His great eyes, which threw out still more rays than His halo, Peter instantly understood: he was sorry he had said too much. What would he not have given that this second mission of the Son of Man upon earth should not take place, and especially that he himself should not have to figure in it! He turned this way and that, quite in despair, with fidgeting hands. "Ah, my Lord! ah, my Lord! And my keys—what shall I do with *them?*" It is true that on so long a journey his heavy bunch would be anything but comfortable. "And my door," he went on—"who will keep it for me?"

On which Jesus smiled, reading to the bottom of his soul, and said: "Leave your keys in the door, Peter. You know very well there's no danger of any one's ever getting in."

He spoke gently, but nobody could have failed to be conscious that there was something implacable in His smile and in His voice.

* * * * * * *

As is told in the Holy Scriptures, the coming of the Son of Man upon earth was announced by signs in the heavens; but for a long time past we crouching mortals had never looked up there. Taken up with our passions, we saw no token of the presence of the Divine Master, nor of that of the old servant who came with Him; all the more that the two travellers had brought with them a change of raiment, and could disguise themselves every way they wished.

None the less, in the first town they came to,

just the night before a famous ruffian called Sanguinarias, the author of dreadful crimes, was to be put to death, the workmen employed in knocking up the stakes of justice in the night were surprised to see among them, lending a hand in the torch-light, two companions who had come from nobody knew where, one of them gallant and easy, like the bastard of a prince, with a fine forked beard and eyes like jewels, the other already bent, with a kindly, drowsy face, and two long scars in runnels on his crumpled cheeks. Then in the early dawn, when the scaffold was up, and the people and the authorities were ranged round for the execution, the two strangers had vanished, leaving the whole machinery so wondrously bewitched that when the condemned man was stretched upon the plank, the blade—a blade well sharpened, steel of the right brand—came down twenty times, one after the other, without making so much as an impression on his skin.

You see from here the picture: the bewilderment of the burgesses, the wild shudder of the crowd, the executioner knocking his assistants about and tearing his sweat-moistened hair, with Sanguinarias himself—the vagabond was, of course, from Beaucaire, and added to all his evil propensities a diabolical conceit—Sanguinarias, greatly vexed, twisting his black bull neck this way and that in the yoke, and crying: "Curse me! what in the world's the matter with me? Ain't I put together like other people?"

Then, at the end of the end, you see the constables obliged to carry the wretch off by force, and thrust him back into his cell, while the howling crowd dances about the demolished scaffold, flaming and crackling up to the sky like a bonfire on an anniversary.

From that time forth, in that city and throughout the civilized world, a spell was cast upon the supreme decrees of justice. The sword of the law refused to cut, and as death is the only thing that murderers fear, soon a perfect deluge of crime flowed over the earth; the streets and the roads ceased to be possible for terrified, decent people; and in the penitentiaries, crammed to the roof, the cutthroats grew fat on good juicy meats, smashed the faces of their warders in with their boot heels, gouged out their eyes with the thumb, or else, simply from curiosity, amused themselves with unscrewing the unfortunate creatures' heads, to see what they had inside.

In the presence of the awful havoc caused by the disarming of justice, it struck poor St. Peter that every one concerned had had about enough, so that with a heart swollen with pity, and a good big hypocritical laugh of conciliation, he remarked:

"The lesson has answered, Master, and I think they'll remember. Shouldn't you say we might go up again? Because, let me tell you, I'm afraid I may be wanted in a certain place."

The Son of Man gave His pale and beautiful smile. "Remember," He said, with a lifted finger, "what Christ put together Christ also can destroy!"

On which Peter reflected, hanging his head,

"I said too much, poor children—I said too much!"

They found themselves at this time on fertile slopes, at the foot of which a rich imperial city, as far as the eye could see, stretched away its domes, its terraces, the lace-work of its belfries, and the towers and spires of cathedrals, on which crosses of every shape, in marble and gold, glittered in the peaceful sunset.

"I hope this lot have enough convents and churches to be saved!" the good old man went on, trying to turn away the wrath of the Lord. "It's pleasant to see *this*, at any rate!"

But you know that what Jesus despises above all things is the hypocritical, sumptuous worship of the Pharisees—churches where people go to mass because it's the fashion, convents that make syrups and chocolate—so that He quickened His step without replying, and, the crops being very high, nothing was seen of the dreadful destroyer, as the pair came down, but a little bundle of clothes swinging at the end of a pedestrian stick.

Well, then, there lived in the city they now entered an old, old emperor, the senior member of the company of princes of Europe, as he was the most powerful and the most just—the one who kept war chained to the axles of his cannon, and, by persuasion or force, prevented the nations from tearing each other to pieces.

So long as he should be there, the tacit agreement between dog and wolf, that the sheep might browse unmolested, would hold; but after that, to a certainty, you would have to stand from under. This is why the whole world cherished the life of the good emperor; there was not a single mother who would not have been ready to open her veins to make his blood ruddier and richer.

Yet, all of a sudden, this love was turned to hate, for an infernal password went about—

"Let's kill him. He's the good tyrant, the most execrable of all, since he leaves us not even the right to rebel!"

So, beneath the imperial palace, undermined and dynamited, in the darkness of the cellars, where the conspirators, up to their middles in water, played their game, I leave you to guess what mysterious companion, with shining eyes, urged on the work of death, closing all hearts to fear and to pity, and, when the blow was dealt, shouting out the supreme hurrah.

As for the poor emperor, alas, no great trace of him was found in the ruins—only a few singed tufts of his beard, and a hand of justice twisted by the flames. Unmuzzled war began straightway to howl; the sky grew black with the ravens gathered together from the ends of the earth; the world settled down, as if forever, to the great business of killing.

* * *

While the nations were putting an end to each other by their abominable engines, while on all quarters of the horizon the taken cities flamed like torches, on the roads blocked up with fleeing cattle, with carts without drivers, along the fields lying fallow, beside the rivers red with blood, the vineyards and harvests unmercifully murdered, Jesus, with

His cheerful step, His wallet on His shoulder, and at His heels the good saint who tried in vain to move Him—Jesus held His course to a distant country, which enjoyed the teachings of a famous doctor of the name of Mr. Mauve.

This Mr. Mauve, a great healer of men and of beasts, directing as he liked all the forces of nature, had very nearly found the secret for prolonging human life; he had indeed just all but put his hand on it, when one night, through the clumsiness of a new assistant, whom he had just taken into his laboratory, and who was never seen again, several jars filled with subtle poisons were left uncorked, so that in the morning Mr. Mauve fell asphyxiated as soon as he opened his door.

This accident scarcely led to the prolongation of human life; quite the contrary, for the learned gentleman had made it his business to collect for study a host of ancient scourges, extraordinary leprosies of Egypt and of the Middle Ages, of which the germs, escaping from the retorts, spread themselves over the world and filled it with desolation. There were showers of toads, pestilential and ignoble, as in the days of the Hebrews; there were fevers — yellow, malignant, quartern, tertian, intermittent — and plagues and typhoids, a host of lost diseases grafted on a host of modern ones, and others, too, that had never been seen; so that among the people all this took the name of Mr. Mauve's disease.

Heaven keep you, my dear children, from any such fearful complaint!

The bones melted like glass, the muscles came off in shreds. People suffered so that they ceased to groan; the dying fell before death into bits, and turned into a mere mess by the road-sides, so that the scavengers had not shovels and carts enough to pick them up.

"Bravo! It's a good job done!" said St. Peter, in a jolly voice, through which you might have felt the tears. "So now, Master, mightn't we go up home again? I begin to feel a sort of sinking."

Jesus knew very well that this sort of sinking covered a great pity for the humans.

* * * * * * *

So now, pursuing his way without answering, and trudging across the country with his old servant, by the glimmer of a little pink, greenish dawn, he suddenly heard, through the call of the cocks and the lowing of beasts—all the first vague sounds that greet the day—a strange human cry, the wail of a woman, rising in great waves, in spasms, now loud enough to rend the sky, now sinking into a long, soft moan—the moan that those who have heard it once can never mistake. In the coming of the day a creature was coming into the world. Jesus stopped and mused. If they kept on being born, of what use was it to destroy them? Looking about for the thatched cabin from which the cry issued, he raised his white hand in a threat.

"Pity, Master, pity for the little ones!" sobbed poor St. Peter.

But the Lord bade him be comforted.

To this child of the breast, as to all who should henceforth be born upon earth, he had made a gift of welcome. Peter was afraid to ask him what it might be; but I, my friends, can tell you what it was. Jesus had given them, the poor little lambs, the gift of experience, and it was to be a very terrible thing.

Reflect that, up to that time, when a man died, the man's experience had died with him. Now, in consequence of this endowment of Jesus, there arose such a thing as experience accumulated. Children were born old and sad and discouraged. As soon as their eyes opened they discovered the end of all things, and people began to see such an abominable thing as the suicide of infants.

And yet all this was still not enough; the accursed race refused to be extinguished—insisted on living in spite of everything.

Therefore, to finish it off sooner, Christ took from men the taste for love; women ceased to be beautiful for them; and for women, men ceased to be lordly, intelligent, and bold. It was the end of all delight, and also the end of all noble sacrifice. There was no sort of joy left for the dwellers on earth; they asked for nothing but forgetfulness of everything; they aspired to nothing but utter sleep. Oh, to sleep, to stop thinking, to stop suffering!

So, you see, our poor humanity was in a very

bad way, and wouldn't have much longer to go, for the indefatigable exterminator drove on his work still faster and faster. He kept roaming all over the world, like a pilgrim with a wallet; and his companion followed him, tremendously tired and bent, with the two furrows of his tears growing deeper and deeper in his cheeks, crying "Mercy! mercy!" when the Master let loose in their track volcanoes and cyclones and earthquakes.

When he had worked off the civilized races, the pair passed into the other parts of the globe.

Now one fine morning—it was the Feast of the Assumption—as Jesus walked the water, treading the waves as he is shown us in Scripture, he reached the middle of the isles of Oceanica, the very same regions of the Pacific that we traverse at this moment.

As he came on and on there was wafted to him on the breeze, from a clump of islands all greenery, a sound of voices of women and children singing the songs of Provence.

"Gracious!" cried St. Peter; "you might take them for the tunes of Tarascon!"

Jesus half looked round at him: "Aren't they rather bad Christians, those Tarasconians?"

"Oh, dear Master, they've got a good deal better lately," the good saint hastened to reply, fearing lest, at a sign from the Divine hand, the island they were approaching might be swallowed up in the deep. This island, as you will have guessed, was none other than Port Tarascon. The inhabitants were celebrating the Feast of the Assumption with a pompous procession around its shores. It was a procession, my children, of the good old sort, of the days when we really believed.

First came the penitents, all the penitents—the blue and the black and the gray, those of every color—preceded by little bells that mingled their notes of crystal and silver. After the penitents walked the sisterhoods of women, dressed in white, and covered with long veils, like the saints of Paradise. Then came the old banners, carried so high that the figures of the saints, with their halos woven in gold in the silken tissues, seemed to have come down from heaven and alighted on the heads of the crowd. The Holy Sacrament advanced with a slow step under its canopy of red velvet, surmounted with great plumes, alongside of which little choristers carried, on the ends of long gilded poles, big green lanterns lighted with a little flickering flame. And all the people of the island followed, young and old, men and women, all chanting and praying.

You could see the procession unroll itself, far away, in a long line, now on the strand, now on the sides of the hills, then over their tops, where the great censers, perpetually swinging, left light blue fumes in the sun. Immensely moved, St. Peter murmured, "Oh, how very lovely!"

He looked at Jesus askance, not hoping to bend him after so many vain attempts; but, seeing that Christ had stopped, erect, on the crest of the waves, he cried once more, in a voice of supplication, "Mercy, mercy at least for these, Lord!"

The Son of Man hesitated a moment; then he remembered that the elect of Port Tarascon were alone worthy to repeople the earth. He raised his pale sweet face, and in the stillness of the pacified sea, with a strong voice that filled all creation, he cried out to heaven, "Father, Father, a respite!"

And through the clear spaces the Father and the Son understood each other without another word.

Brother Bataillet had reached this point in his parable, and the audience, so great was their emotion, sat still in their places, when, all of a sudden, from the lookout of the *Tootoopumpum*, Captain Scrapouchinat shouted: "Our island is in sight, your Excellency! Port Tarascon's in sight! In another hour we shall be at anchor!"

Then all the world jumped up, and there was a tremendous chatter.

VI.

"WHAT the devil is this? Nobody down to meet us!" said Tartarin, after the tumult of the first cries of joy had subsided.

Doubtless the ship had not yet been seen from the shore.

They must call their friends' attention. Three cannon-shots boomed over two long islands of a greasy green, a rheumatic green, between which the steamer had begun to advance.

All eyes were turned towards the nearer shore, a narrow strip of sand only a few yards wide, beyond which nothing was visible but certain slopes, all covered, from the summit to the sea, with landslides of dark verdure.

When the echo of the cannon had ceased to rumble, a great stillness settled again on these strange, rather grewsome islands. Still no one could be seen, and what was even more startling than the inexplicable absence of human beings was that there was not a sign of a harbor, or a fort, or a town, or piers, or ship-yards, or anything else.

Tartarin turned round to Scrapouchinat, who was already giving the order to cast anchor:

"Are you quite sure, Captain?"

The irascible seaman replied with a wicked look. Was he quite sure? The devil take him! He knew his trade, perhaps; he knew how to sail his ship!

"Pascalon, go and fetch me the map of the island," cried Tartarin.

He possessed, happily, a map of the settlement, drawn on a very large scale, in which capes, gulfs, rivers, mountains, and even the very position of the principal monuments of the city were minutely noted.

This map was immediately spread out, and Tartarin, surrounded by all, began to study it and to trace the different features with his finger.

It was the place indeed: here the island of Port Tarascon; the other island opposite; there the promontory, thingumbob, quite right. To the left the coral reefs, perfectly. What was the matter, then? Where were they? Where was Port Tarascon, and where were its inhabitants?

Bashfully, stammering a little, Pascalon suggested that perhaps under it all was a practical

joke of Bompard's; he was so well known at Tarascon for his merry ways.

Bompard possibly, but Bézuquet—a man of all prudence, of all gravity—never! "Besides," added Tartarin, "let your ways be as merry as they will, you can't put a town and a harbor and a careening dock up your sleeves."

On the shore, with the telescope, they did see something like a sort of shed, but even this was not very plain. The coral reefs made it impossible for the ship to go near, and at that distance everything was muddled in the black verdure of the vegetation.

Greatly mystified, they all stared, quite ready to land, with their parcels in their hands. The old dowager of Aigueboulide carried her little foot-warmer herself, and her nodding head made her look more astonished than the others. Amid the general stupefaction, the Governor in person was heard to murmur, under his breath, "It's really most extraordinary!"

But suddenly he took a stand. "Captain, have the long-boat manned. Commandant, sound the rally for your troops."

While the bugle was going, "tarata-tarata-taratata!" and Bravida was getting the militia together, Tartarin, with characteristic ease of manner, cheered up the ladies: "Don't be afraid. Everything will certainly be explained."

And to the men—to those who were not to go with him: "We shall be back in an hour. Wait for us here. Let no one move."

No one would have moved for the world. They all surrounded him, saying what he said, "Yes, your Excellency, everything will be explained; certainly it will." At this moment Tartarin seemed to them immense.

The Governor took his place in the long-boat, with his secretary, Pascalon, and his chaplain, Brother Bataillet, and with Bravida, Tournatoire, Escourbaniès, and the militia, all armed to the teeth with sabres, hatchets, revolvers, and rifles, to say nothing of the famous Winchester, the thirty-two shooter.

As they drew nearer to the silent shore, where nothing stirred, they made out an old landing-stage of rafters and planks, standing in a stagnant pool, and all overgrown with moss. It was impossible that this object should be the breakwater on which the natives had come to meet the passengers of the *Farandole*. Farther on appeared a species of old shanty, its windows closed with iron shutters painted in red lead, which threw a bloody gleam into the dead water. It was covered with a roof of planks, dislocated, seamed with great crevices which had been patched up with a tattered tarpaulin.

As soon as they landed they visited this shanty. The inside, like the outside, was in a lamentable state of decay. Great slices of sky peeped in through the roof; the flooring, warped into a hump, was crumbling away into powder; enormous lizards flitted through all the chinks; the walls were overrun with black beetles; slimy toads slobbered in the corners. Tartarin, going in first, had almost stepped on a serpent as big as his arm.

From the remains of some partitions still standing, they perceived that the interior had been divided into narrow compartments, like little bath-houses, or stalls in a stable. The place reeked with the smell of damp and mould, something sickly, that turned the stomach. There were only two things to indicate that it had ever been inhabited—a few tin boxes lying about the ground, familiar receptacles of the well-known preserves of the Abbey of Pampérigouste, and on the boards of one of the cubicles a remnant of the words Bézu. . . . Drug. . . . The rest had disappeared, devoured by mildew; but one had not to be a great scholar to guess "Bézuquet, Druggist."

"I see what has happened," said Tartarin. "This side of the island proved unhealthy, and after a fruitless attempt to settle they have gone to establish themselves on the other side." Then, in a voice of decision, he ordered the commandant to make a reconnoissance at the head of the troops. Bravida was to push up to the top of the mountain, whence he would explore the country, and certainly see the smoke of the roofs of the city.

"As soon as you have established communication, you will notify us by a loud volley."

As for himself, he would remain there, at headquarters, with his secretary, his chaplain, and a few others.

Bravida and his lieutenant, Escourbaniès, drew up their men and set off. The troops advanced in good order, but the rising ground, covered with a kind of sea-weedy moss, on which their feet slipped, rendered the march so difficult that the ranks were not slow to fall apart. They crossed a little rivulet, on the edge of which lingered some vestiges of a washing-place, a clothes-beater forgotten, the whole greened over with the invading, smothering moss that cropped up everywhere. This was probably the famous river!

A little farther they recognized the traces of another structure, which seemed to have been a sort of rough citadel, also muffled in moss and in the exuberance of the forest the gigantic roots that burst through the ground and sprawled over the slopes.

What completed the disarray of the poor soldiers was to encounter hundreds of holes, very near each other, treacherously covered over with the vegetation of brambles and creepers. Several men sank into them, with a great rattle of arms and equipment, frightening away by their fall a multitude of the same big lizards that they had seen in the shanty. These holes were not very deep; they were only slight excavations dug in rows. Bravida made the remark that they resembled a deserted quarry.

"Or rather a deserted cemetery," Escourbaniès replied—"a cemetery from which there has been a flitting."

There were, in fact, traces of bones, and what gave him this idea were certain vague suggestions of crosses, formed of intertwined branches, now leafy again, restored to nature, and looking like stems and shoots of the wild grape.

After a painful scramble through thick underbrush they at last reached the summit. There they breathed a healthier air, freshened by the breeze and charged with whiffs from the sea. Before them stretched away a great bare moor, after which the ground gradually sank again to the sea. It was over there that the town would be; and indeed one of the soldiers, pointing his finger, showed them in the distance the curl of rising smoke. At the same time Escourbaniès broke out joyously, "Listen! listen! the tambourines! the national reel!"

There was no mistake about it, the vibration of the tune of the farandole was perceptible in the light air. Port Tarascon was coming to meet them.

They saw them already, the people from the town, a crowd flocking up yonder, at the top of the ascent, the extremity of the plateau.

"Cracky!" cried Bravida, suddenly; "you'd say they were savages!"

At the head of the band, in front of the tambourines, danced a great lean black, in a sailor's jersey, with blue spectacles on his nose and brandishing a tomahawk.

The two bodies had now stopped, and were watching each other from a distance. Suddenly Bravida burst into a loud laugh: "This is too much! Ah, the buffoon!" And thrusting his sabre back into its scabbard, he began to run forward. His men called him back: "Commandant! Commandant!"

But he never listened to them; he kept on running. He had recognized Bompard, and shouted, as he approached him: "That's played out, old chap. It's too much like it—too true to nature!"

The other continued to dance and whirl his weapon; and when the unhappy Bravida perceived that he had before him not his friend Bompard, but a veritable barbarian, it was too late to dodge the terrible head-cracking blow which smashed in his cork helmet, dashed out his poor little brains, and stretched him stiff upon the ground.

At the same time burst forth a tempest of dreadful cries, while a cloud of arrows flew through the air. Seeing their commandant fall, the soldiers had instinctively and precipitately fired; then they had scuttled away without perceiving that the savages had done as much on the other side.

From below Tartarin had heard all the firing. "They've established communication," he joyously announced.

But his joy was turned to stupor when he saw the little army come rushing back in disorder, leaping through the woods, some without hats, others without shoes, all uttering the same appalling cry, "The savages! the savages!" There was a moment of unspeakable panic. The long-boat made for the open, pulling away like mad. The Governor ran up and down the shore, crying, "Keep cool! oh, keep cool!" with chattering teeth, the note of the sea-gull in distress. It only added to the universal scare.

On the narrow strip of sand the confusion of this scramble for life lasted a few moments; but as no one knew in what direction to flee, they after a little came together again. As no savage showed himself, they regained a degree of confidence, and were able to recognize and question each other.

"And the commandant?"

"Dead!"

When Escourbaniès had described Bravida's fatal blunder, Tartarin exclaimed: "Unhappy Placidius! But, I must say," he added, "what an imprudence! In an enemy's country, not to throw out skirmishers!"

He immediately ordered sentinels to be posted. The soldiers designated walked away slowly, two by two, for no one wished to remain alone, often turning their heads, and plainly determined not to leave the body of the troops too far off. Then the others gathered in council, while Tournatoire gave his attention to the wounds of a private who had received a poisoned arrow, and was swelling up from minute to minute in the most extraordinary fashion.

Tartarin, in council, was the first to address his companions.

"Before everything," he wisely said, "we must avoid the shedding of blood." And he proposed to send Brother Bataillet to shake a palm-leaf in the distance, so as to get a notion of what was going on in the enemy's quarter. "Your Reverence will see what the savages are doing, and what has become of our compatriots."

But Brother Bataillet loudly protested. He was not in the least of that opinion. "Oh, come, now—a palm-leaf! I should greatly prefer your Winchester and its thirty-two shots!"

"All right; if his Reverence won't go, I'll go myself," the Governor declared. "Only, my

9

dear chaplain, you must come with me, for I don't know enough of the Papuan tongue—"

"But I assure you I don't know it either."

"The deuce you don't! What, then, have you been teaching me these last three months? All those lessons that I took from you on the voyage—what language was that, if you please?"

Brother Bataillet, like the fine old Tarasconian that he was, got out of it by pleading that he knew the Papuan of the other part, but not the Papuan of that part.

All of a sudden, during this discussion, broke out a new alarm; firing was heard in the direction of the sentinels, and from the depths of the wood issued a voice which cried, in the well-known accent of home, "Don't shoot!—in Heaven's name, don't shoot!"

A minute later there might have been seen to bound from the thicket the queerest of all creatures, hideously tattooed in vermilion and black, so that he looked as if he were clad from head to feet in the variegated tights of a clown. It was none other than Chemist-physician Bézuquet.

"Bless us and save us—Bézuquet!"

"Why, how d'ye do, Bézuquet?"

"How does it happen—"

"But where are the others?"

"And the city, and the harbor, and the shipyard?"

"Of the town," the druggist replied, pointing out the shanty before mentioned, "behold what remains! Of the inhabitants, behold also!" And he pointed to himself. "But before everything, do quickly put something over me to hide the abominations with which these villains have covered me!"

Sure enough, all the foulest things conceivable

to the imagination of barbarians in delirium had been pricked in color into his wretched skin.

Escourbaniès handed him his own mantle of Grandee of the first class, and after the unfortunate man had refreshed himself with a good swig of brandy, he began, with the accent he had not lost and the Tarasconian elocution: "If you were painfully surprised this morning to find that the city of Port Tarascon has never existed but on the map and in your fond imaginations, think whether we, of the first and second batches, when we arrived in the *Farandole* and the *Lucifer*—"

"Excuse me if I interrupt you," said Tartarin, who saw the sentinels on the edge of the wood giving signs of uneasiness. "I think it will be wiser if you tell us your story on board. We may be surprised here by the cannibals."

"Not at all. Your firing has scared them half to death. They've all rushed away; they've quitted the island, and I've taken advantage of it to escape."

"Never mind," insisted Tartarin; "it's much better that you should tell us what you have to tell in the presence of the Grand Council. The situation is too grave."

They hailed the long-boat, which from the beginning of the flurry had remained timorously aloof, and they regained the ship, where the rest were awaiting in anguish the result of the reconnoissance ashore.

VII.

Grewsome indeed were the tribulations of the first tenants of Port Tarascon as related in the saloon of the *Tootoopumpum* before the Grand Council, a body composed of the Ancients, the Governor, the Commissioners, the Grandees of the first and second classes, and the captain of the ship and his staff.

On the deck the passengers, especially the ladies, quivered with impatience and curiosity, but they could hear nothing but the steady hum of Bézuquet's deep bass, and the quick outbreaks of interruption proceeding from Tartarin or Brother Bataillet.

In the first place, as soon as they started, when the *Farandole* had scarcely got out of the Bay of Marseilles, there had been a bad omen. Bompard, Provisional Governor and chief of the expedition, abruptly seized with a strange ailment, of a contagious nature, as he declared, had caused himself to be put ashore at the

Chateau d'If, handing over his gubernatorial powers to Bézuquet. What luck that fellow had had, too! You might think he had guessed everything that was in store for them. At Suez they had found the *Lucifer* in too bad a state to continue her journey, and had transferred her cargo to the *Farandole*, already too full.

Lord, what they had suffered from the heat on that blessed ship, crammed from the deck to the hold! If they remained above, they melted in the sun; if they went below, they were squeezed and smothered to death. It was so hot that they could keep nothing on. The cabins were a furnace, a perfect hell!

All this was so bad that on reaching Port Tarascon, in spite of the disappointment of finding nothing whatever—neither town, nor port, nor pier, nor buildings of any kind—they had felt such a need of breathing again, stretching themselves, and getting out of each other's way, that their disembarkation, even on a desert strand, had seemed to them a real relief. In the first moments it had been a delight merely to be able to walk about. They even made a few jokes. Notary Cambalalette, Assessor of Taxes, who was always up to something droll, asked what he would have to assess in a country where there was no property to hold. Later had come their reflections on the gravity of the situation.

"We decided then," said Bézuquet, "to send the ship to Sydney to bring back building materials, and transmit you the despairing message that you of course received."

The narrator was interrupted on all sides by protestations.

"A despairing message?"

"What message?"

"We received no message!"

Tartarin's voice rose above the others: "In the way of a message, my dear sir, we only received the one describing the splendid reception offered you by the indigenous population, and the *Te Deum* chanted in the cathedral. Go on; everything will be explained."

The council repeated in chorus: "Yes, yes—everything will be explained!"

"Go on, Ferdinand," added Tartarin, turning again to the druggist.

"I resume," said Bézuquet. He resumed accordingly, and his story became more and more dismal.

They had gone bravely to work. Possessing agricultural implements, they began to clear and plant, only the soil was so bad that nothing came — nothing on earth would grow. The most pertinacious were soon convinced that there was nothing to be done. And then the rains—

A cry from the auditory again interrupted Bézuquet: "You say it rains?"

"Do I say so? Why, more than at Lyons! Ten months of the year!"

Consternation descended. Instinctively all eyes were turned to the port-holes, through which they discerned a dense mist, the clouds sticking fast to the black green, the rheumatic green, of the hills. Every one was struck with the melancholy of the scene.

"Go on, Ferdinand, go on," Tartarin kept saying.

So Ferdinand went on. With the perpetual rains, the stagnant floods that covered the country, fevers and agues had lost no time in making their appearance. The cemetery was promptly inaugurated, and pining and "sinking" were added to disease. Even the pluckiest lost all courage for work, so flabby they became in the soaking climate.

They spent all their time in the big house, feeding on preserves, and also on lizards, on serpents brought over by the Papuans encamped on the other side of the isle.

Father Vezole had undertaken to convert the daughter of King Nagonko. An excellent man, this Father Vezole, and full of good intentions; but perhaps it was not quite right of him to try to establish this regular intercourse with the natives. The latter, essentially crafty, had little by little wriggled into the settlement. They came in more and more, always on the pretext of bringing the produce of their fishing and their hunting. Our friends were not mistrustful of them, and grew accustomed to their presence,

so that the simplest precautions were neglected.

So one fine night it befell that the Papuans broke into the big house; slipping like so many devils through the door, through the windows, and the apertures of the roof, they got hold of all the arms, massacred those who attempted to resist, and carried off all the others to their camp.

For a month there was an uninterrupted succession of horrible feasts. The prisoners, each in his turn, were clubbed to death on the head, then roasted or baked in the earth on hot stones, like sucking pigs, and devoured by these cannibal savages.

The cry of horror uttered by the whole council carried dismay even up to the deck, and it was in a still feebler voice that the Governor said, once more, "Go on, Ferdinand."

The poor druggist had in this way seen each

of his companions disappear, one by one. Gentle Father Vezole accepted death with a smile of resignation, with his "God be praised!" on his lips. Notary Cambalalette, so gay, such a jolly rascal, was sacrificed the last.

"And the monsters compelled me to eat a bit of him, poor Cambalalette!" added Bézuquet, shuddering still with this reminiscence.

In the silence that followed these terrible words, the bilious Costecalde, all yellow and grinning with rage, turned to the Governor.

"You told us, nevertheless, you wrote, and caused to be written, that there were no anthropophagi!"

And as the Governor, overwhelmed, hung

his head and held his tongue, Bézuquet replied:

"No anthropophagi? Why, every mother's son is one. They know no greater treat than human flesh—especially ours, the white kind, the very quality produced at Tarascon—to that degree that after having devoured the living they passed on to the dead. You've seen the former cemetery? Nothing is left there—not a bone; they've picked and scraped and scoured, as you scour the plates when the soup is good, or when you sit down to some jolly garlic stew."

"But yourself, Bézuquet?" asked a Grandee of the first class. "How came it that you were spared?"

The ex-apothecary supposed that by reason of living among bottles and jars, of soaking in pharmaceutic products—mint, arsenic, arnica, and ipecac—his flesh had gradually acquired a herbaceous flavor which probably was not to their taste; unless indeed, on the contrary, precisely on account of this druggy aroma, they had been keeping him for the sweet dish—the tidbit of the end.

When he had concluded his story they all looked at each other a moment; then the Marquis des Espazettes inquired,

"Very well, now, what are we going to do?"

"What do you mean—what are you going to do?" said Scrapouchinat, with his customary snarl. "You're not in any case going to stay here, I suppose?"

They broke out on all sides: "Ah, no, indeed—most certainly not!"

"Though I've been paid only to bring you," the captain continued, "I'm ready to take home those who want to go."

At this moment all the defects of his disposition were overlooked. His companions forgot that he regarded them only as green monkeys, fit to be shot. They surrounded him; they congratulated him; they stretched out their hands to him. In the midst of the noise Tartarin's voice was suddenly heard, in a tone of high dignity:

"You will do what you like, gentlemen; for myself, I remain. I have my mission of Governor. I must carry it out."

"Governor of what?—since there's nothing to govern!" Scrapouchinat yelled.

The others backed him up: "Yes, indeed, the captain's right: there *is* nothing to govern!"

But Tartarin rose over the tumult: "The Duc de Mons has my word, gentlemen."

"He's a swindler, your Duc de Mons," said

Bézuquet. "I always suspected it, even before I had the proof."

"And where is it, your proof?"

"Not in my pocket, alas!" And, with a recurrence of modesty, the ex-apothecary drew closer round him the mantle of Grandee of the first class which protected his bepictured nudity. "What is very certain is that Bompard in his last moments said to me, 'Look out for the Belgian: he's a humbug!' If he had been able to speak he would have said more; but his cruel weakness left him no strength."

Besides, what better proof could they have than the accursed island itself, barren and pestilential, which the humbug in question had sent them to clear and populate? What better proof than the false despatches?

The liveliest movement broke out in the council; they all talked at once, approving Bézuquet, and overwhelming the duke with abusive epithets:

"A liar! A swindler! A dirty Belgian!"

Tartarin, heroic, boldly confronted them all: "Until the contrary is proved, I reserve my opinion upon his Grace."

"His Grace, forsooth! Our opinion's formed: a common thief!"

"He may have been imprudent, imperfectly informed himself—"

"Don't defend him. He deserves penal servitude."

"For myself, appointed Governor of Port Tarascon, at Port Tarascon I remain."

"Remain alone, then."

"Alone, so be it, if you all forsake me. I will populate alone, but I will not expose myself to the ignominy of going home. Only leave me the implements of tillage—"

"But since I tell you that there's nothing to till, and that nothing will grow!" cried Bézuquet.

"Isn't it because you set wrongly about it, Ferdinand?"

Then Scrapouchinat flew into a rage, and smote the council table with his fists. "The man's mad! I don't know what keeps me from carrying him aboard by force, and from shooting him like a green monkey if he resists!"

"Try it, then—the devil take you!"

Pale with anger, with a threatening gesture, Brother Bataillet had risen erect at Tartarin's side.

This exchange of violent words had raised the tumult to its climax. In the midst of it could be heard a cross-fire of Tarasconian expressions: "You're wanting in sense. You don't talk straight. You say things that had better not be said."

Heaven knows how it all would have ended without the intervention of Lawyer Franquebalme, the Commissioner of Justice.

This Franquebalme was the most fluent of lawyers, flowering over his arguments with many a whensoever and wheresoever, many an "on the one hand" and "on the other hand"; so that his speeches were as built up, as cemented and solid, as one of our old Roman aqueducts. A fine old Latin sage, fed on Ciceronian periods, he let you always have the right and the wrong of it, and, as he said, the why of the wherefore.

He took advantage of the first lull to begin a harangue, and in long, fair phrases, which he rolled off without end, he emitted the opinion that the passengers should be consulted, should cast their vote on going or staying. They should hold a plebiscitum, voting yes or no. On the one side, those who wanted to stay should stay, while on the other those who wanted to go should go. The ship would carry them off after its carpenters had rebuilt the big house and the citadel.

This motion of Franquebalme's made the

whole company unanimous. It was instantly adopted, and they began to vote without delay.

A great agitation broke out on deck and in the cabins as soon as it became known what they were doing. Nothing was heard but lamentations and groans. All the poor people had put their substance into purchases of land—the famous cheap acres! Were they then to lose everything, to give up the farms and estates they had paid for, their hope of settling and flourishing? These considerations of interest urged them to vote for staying; but, on the other hand, a single look at the dreadful landscape threw them into hesitation. The sight of the ruins of the big house, of the black, soaking greenery, behind which they imagined the desert and the savages, the prospect of being eaten like Cambalalette—nothing in all this was encouraging, and their desires reverted to the sweet land of Provence, so imprudently quitted, where there were neither deserts nor cannibals.

The emigrants swarmed over the ship like so many ants whose hillock has been disturbed. The old nodding dowager roamed up and down the deck like a lost soul, without letting go either her foot-warmer or her parrot. In the midst of the hubbub of the discussions preceding the ballot several disputes occurred, and nothing was heard on every side but imprecations against the Belgian, the dirty Belgian! Oh, it was no longer his Grace the Duke! The dirty Belgian!—they said it with clinched fists and grinding teeth.

In spite of everything, out of the thousand Tarasconians on the ship a hundred and fifty elected to remain with Tartarin. It must be said that the majority were high dignitaries, and that the Governor had promised to leave them their positions and titles.

Then there rose fresh discussions about the division of the food between those going and those staying.

"You'll revictual at Sydney," said those who were staying to those who were going.

"You'll hunt and you'll fish," replied the latter to the former. "Why in the world do you require such a lot of preserves?"

The Tarasque, moreover, gave rise to terrible debates. Should she go back to Tarascon? Should she remain with the settlement?

The dispute grew very hot. Scrapouchinat threatened several times to put Brother Batail-let to the sword.

Lawyer Franquebalme, to maintain peace, had to become afresh the persuasive Nestor of the occasion, and intervene with all his legal lore. But he had great difficulty in soothing down several excited spirits, secretly worked upon as they were by the hypocritical Escourbaniès, who only sought to prolong the discord.

Shaggy and shrill, with his motto, borrowed from the mother-land, of "Let's make a noise!" the lieutenant of the militia was so intensely Southern that he was black with it; with his tightly crinkled hair, he had not only the color of the ace of spades, he had also the cowardice, the desire to please, that have been known to go with the complexion—always dancing the hornpipe of success before the stronger, before the captain on shipboard, surrounded with his crew, or before Tartarin on land, in the midst of the troops. To each of these he explained differently the reasons that determined him to remain at Port Tarascon, saying to Scrapouchinat, "I'm staying because my wife expects to be confined." And to Tartarin, "Nothing on earth would induce me to make another trip with that perfect vandal."

The Tarasque was left with the people of the ship, in exchange for a small cannon and a long-boat.

Tartarin had extracted provisions, arms, and tool-chests piece by piece.

For several days there reigned between the ship and the shore a perpetual going and coming of small boats laden with a thousand things —guns, preserves, boxes of sardines and of the delicate tunny, biscuits, supplies of swallow tarts, and potted pears.

At the same time the axe rang out in the

woods, where there was a great havoc made among the trees for the repair of the big house and the citadel. The loud notes of the bugle mingled with the sound of the hatchet and the hammer. During the day the troops, under arms, kept guard over the workers, for fear of

an attack of the savages; during the night they encamped on the strand, round the watch-fires —"in order to get used to the hardships of campaigning," said Tartarin.

When everything was ready on shore, the ship prepared to put off. The hour of separation had arrived, but the parting was rather cool. Those who were going were jealous of those who remained; which didn't prevent them, however, from saying, with a little sneering smile, "If you get on pretty well, just drop us a line, and we'll come back."

On their side, in spite of their assumption of confidence in the future, those who remained envied those who were going.

After it had weighed anchor, the ship fired a salvo from its guns, and the little cannon, handled by Brother Bataillet, replied from the shore. Meanwhile Escourbaniès played on his clarinet the familiar air, "A happy journey, dear Dumollet!"

Never mind; in spite of the irony of this farewell, there was a great emotion at the bottom of every heart, and when the *Tootoopumpum* had rounded the promontory, when she had finally disappeared from sight, the waters she had quitted, now empty and larger, seemed to them all to have a woful extent.

BOOK SECOND.

I.

December 20, *1881.*—I have undertaken to commit to this register the principal events in our annals.

I shall have a lot of trouble, with all the work already on my shoulders; for, as General Commissioner of the different Bureaux, I look after all the administrative papers, and then, as soon as I have a minute to myself, dash off a few verses in our special idiom, for fear the high functionary in my spirit may destroy the national bard.

Never mind. I shall manage to keep everything going. It will be curious some day to follow these first steps in the career of a people. I have spoken to nobody of the work I begin to-day, not even to the Governor.

The first thing to be noted is the happy turn

of affairs since the *Tootoopumpum* left us a week ago. We are getting settled, and the flag of Fort Tarascon, which bears the Tarasque quartered on the French colors, floats from the summit of the citadel.

It is there that the Government is established, by which I mean our Tartarin, the Commissioners, and the Bureaux. The unmarried Commissioners, like myself, like M. Tournatoire, Commissioner of Health, and Brother Bataillet, Grand Chief of Artillery and of the Navy, are lodged at headquarters. Costecalde and Escourbaniès, who are married, eat and sleep in town.

When we say "in town," we mean the general residence, the big house which the carpenters of the *Tootoopumpum* succeeded in putting into fair condition. Around it we have laid out a kind of boulevard, a promenade, to which we have given the pompous name of the "Walk Round." It is quite Tarascon over again. We have already taken the habit of it. We say: "I think I'll go into town this evening. Have you been into town to-day? Suppose we go into town." And it all seems quite natural.

Headquarters are separated from town by the little river, to which we have given the name of

the Little Rhone. This is a sweet memento of home.

From my office, when the window is open, I hear the slapping and beating of the washer-women, though it doesn't go so fast nor sound so sharp as their Tarasconian chatter. I see them leaning over the bank; I hear their songs, their calls to each other; and this little picture, the dialect of home, with its sharp sonorities, putting a bit of scenery into the air, quite recalls and revives the mother-land.

There is only one thing that makes it disagreeable for me at headquarters — the consciousness of the magazine. Our friends left us a great quantity of powder, which, with the culverin, has been deposited in the subcellar of the citadel. There also are our general stores, our supplies of provisions of every description — garlic, preserves, liquids, reserves of weapons, of instruments and tools. The whole thing is carefully bolted and barred, but all the same it rather haunts me, especially at night, to think of our having there under our feet such a lot of explosive and combustible matter, quite enough to blow up the Government and the whole place.

September 25th.—Yesterday Madame Escourbaniès was safely delivered of a fine boy.

He is the first little citizen inscribed on our books. Accordingly we have given him the suggestive name of Miraclete. He has been baptized in great pomp at St. Martha's of the Palms, our little provisional church, constructed of bamboo, with a roof of big leaves.

I had the good-fortune to be godfather, and to have for godmother Mademoiselle Clorinde des Espazettes. She is unfortunately a little tall for me, but *so* pretty; she looked wonderfully fresh and smart under the checkers of light that filtered through the trellis of bamboo and between the gaps of the leafy roof.

The whole city was collected; our good Governor pronounced a few admirable words, moving to us all, and Brother Bataillet brought the ceremony to a close by the recital of one of his charming tales.

The day was treated as a holiday, and work was everywhere suspended. We made a regular fête of it. After the christening came a general stroll on the Walk Round. All the world was in spirits; it seemed as if the new-born babe had brought hope and happiness to the colony. The Government distributed a double ration of tunny and potted pears, and in the evening there was an extra dish on every table. At headquarters we put a wild pig to roast, owing the animal to the skill of the Marquis des Espazettes, the first shot on the island after Tartarin.

When dinner was over, as the Governor went out to smoke, I went with him. He struck me

as so kind and paternal, as we talked together, that I confessed to him my affection for Mademoiselle Clorinde. He smiled; he was already aware of it. He promised me to intercede, and, full of encouraging words, spoke to me of my fine position. It is true that to be General Commissioner of the Bureaux at my age—

Unfortunately the marquise is a Lambesc, very proud of her origin, and I am only a commoner. Of a good family, doubtless; we have nothing to be ashamed of; but we have always lived as plain folk. I have also against me my bashfulness, my slight stutter, and moreover there is a little place on top where my hair is beginning to thin. But I have a spirit and a future.

Oh, if it were only a question of the marquis—deuce of a bit would *he* care, so long as he

can get his sport! It is not like his wife, with her quarterings. Only fancy—an Espazettes! To give you an idea of her pride, all the world, in town, assembles in the evening in the general saloon. It's very pleasant; the ladies bring their knitting, the men take a hand at whist. But Madame des Espazettes is too grand for this, and remains with her daughters in their cubicle, though the place is so tiny that when the ladies change their gown two of them can never do it at once. Very well, the marquise would rather pass her evenings there, receiving "at home," and offering camomile tea and sickly decoctions of herbs to guests who can't sit down, than mingle with the rest, so great is her horror of the Rabblebabble. That will give you an idea.

However, I have the Governor with me, and in spite of everything this gives me hope.

September 29th.—I have not been out for two days, have not budged from my room or my office.

Yesterday the Governor went down into town. He promised me to speak of my little matter, so as to have it to tell me about when he came back. You may think if I waited with impatience! But when he came back he never opened his mouth. What does this mean? I can't imagine, and I didn't venture to question him.

During breakfast he was nervous, and in conversation with his chaplain these words escaped him, "If you come to that, we have too little of the Rabblebabble."

As Madame des Espazettes de Lambesc has always on her lips this contemptuous expression, "the Rabblebabble," I thought that he might have seen her, and that my request had not been acceded to; but I was unable to find out how matters stood, inasmuch as the Governor immediately began to talk of the report of Commissioner Costecalde on the subject of agriculture.

This report has been most dismal. It tells of fruitless attempts of maize, of corn, of carrots, of potatoes, of everything refusing to sprout. There is no vegetable mould, and so much water, with the impervious soil, that all the seed is swamped. In a word, it is what Bézuquet announced, only still more wretched.

I must add that the Commissioner of Agriculture perhaps does his best to push matters to the worst, and present them in the saddest light. Costecalde, in truth, is such an evil spirit! He has always been jealous of Tartarin's glory. I feel that he is animated with sneaking hatred of him.

All the while lunch lasted nothing was talked of but this report. Brother Bataillet, who never goes the longest way round, plumped out a demand for Costecalde's dismissal; but the Governor replied, with his high reason and his habitual moderation, "It is requested of your Reverence not to get started."

On leaving table we passed into Costecalde's private room, and Tartarin went up to him, you know, quite calm. "So, as we were saying, Mr. Commissioner, our cultivation—"

The other, very sour, replied, without wincing, "I have addressed my report to his Excellency."

"Come, come, really, Costecalde, your report's a trifle severe."

Costecalde turned quite yellow. "It's just what it has to be, and if people are not satisfied—"

His eyes flamed, and the insolence rang out in his voice; but Tartarin controlled himself on account of the others who were present.

"Costecalde," he said, with two sparks in his little gray eyes, "I'll have two words with you when we're alone."

It was terrible; the perspiration poured from me.

September 30th.—Oh, these old nobles—what an awful crew!

It's just as I feared; my suit has been scorned by the house of Espazettes. I'm of too humble extraction. I'm authorized to visit there as before, but I'm forbidden to hope.

Devil take it, what are they looking for? Is there a noble in the settlement to whom they can give their Clorinde? They themselves are the only grand people. Do they want to make her an old spinster, like Mademoiselle Tournatoire? Do they want to make her, I mean, a poor wounded heart? For, strictly, I can't compare so lovely a creature to the tall Touareg, who, for the last twenty years or more, has been showing our Tartarin the whites of her eyes, never taking it in that he can't possibly want her, that he means never to marry at all, having taken glory for his bride.

What am I to do? What line can I take? Clorinde loves me enough, I'm sure, to elope with me, and let me seal our union in some other country. But what other country—since we have the bad luck to be on an island?

I could, in a manner, have understood their repudiating me when I was only a druggist's apprentice. But to-day I have a future. To put it in a word, Tartarin delights in me; he has no children; I may dream of almost anything! Who knows but later— It would only be the matter of a transfer of authority. Yes, surely, there are no aspirations forbidden me.

How many others would like to believe I think of *them!* Without going very far, little Miss Franquebalme, a good musician—she "learns" her sisters—is a case in which the

parents would be enchanted if I were to so much as lift my finger.

Despair! despair! This, then, is the consummation of all my dreams, of the brave illusions I framed during those sweet talks on the deck of the *Tootoopumpum*. And since we have been here, what other delicious hours! Must I relinquish joys that are great in spite of being made of little things—evenings passed near her at the window, words exchanged that seem to be nothing and that yet say so much, the accidental contact of our hands when she offers me the cup of camomile, the decoction of herbs?

They are over, those happy days! And to finish me off, it has been raining ever since this morning, raining without a stop, so that everything is blurred and blotted out and drowned muffled in a deadly gray veil.

Ah, Bézuquet told the truth—it does rain at Port Tarascon; it certainly does. The torrents surround us on every side, cage us up behind the fine wires of a cricket-hutch. There's no horizon left, nothing but the rain and the rain. It swamps the land and riddles the ocean, which mixes with the water that falls—all the water that rises in splash and spray.

October 3d.—Yes, the Governor's allusion was happy; we have not quite enough of the Rabble-babble. Rather fewer quarterings of nobility, fewer high dignitaries, and rather more plumbers and masons and slaters and thatchers and carpenters would meet our requirements considerably better.

Last night, with the continual rain, these water-spouts that soak through everything, the roof of the big house burst in, and the city was inundated. The morning has been spent in general bewilderment—complaints on complaints, an incessant rushing to and fro between headquarters and town.

The different bureaux shift the responsibility from one to the other. The Department of Agriculture says it's *our* business, while our department insists that the matter falls within the jurisdiction of the Board of Health; this board, meanwhile, sending the complainants to the Navy, because it's a question of planking and building.

In town they were all furious, up to their knees in water, but declaring that it's all the fault of the "state of things." From this position they refuse to budge, quite indifferent to the conflict of jurisdiction. Meanwhile the great gap has been growing bigger, the water gushing in a cataract from the roof, so that there's nothing to be seen in the cubicles but people squabbling under open umbrellas, and brawling and bawling, and accusing the Government.

Happily we have no lack of umbrellas. There was a tremendous lot of them in our assortment of goods for barter with the savages—almost as many as dog-collars—enormous cotton ones of every color, which we are very glad to have in a country of permanent rain.

Well, to finish about the inundation, a brave

girl, a servant-maid belonging to Mademoiselle Tournatoire, scrambled up on the roof and nailed over it a sheet of zinc, extracted for the purpose from the emporium. The Governor directs me to write her a letter of felicitation.

If I mention this incident here, it is because

the occasion has made the weakness of our colony so conspicuous.

The administration is excellent, zealous, even complicated, thoroughly French; but for colonizing purposes we simply want hands. The scribbled paper is out of proportion to the strong arms.

I'm also struck with another thing, the fact that each of our big-wigs has been intrusted with the kind of work for which he's least suited and least prepared. Costecalde, the armorer, for instance, who has spent his life in the midst of pistols and rifles, the implements of the chase, is Commissioner of Agriculture. Escourbaniès hadn't his like for the manufacture of the blessed Arles sausage; but since poor Bravida's accident he has become Commissioner of War and head of the Levies. Brother Bataillet has taken the Artillery and the Navy, because he knows how to sail a boat and fire a cannon; but, after all, what he knows much better is to say mass and tell us stories.

In town it is the same thing. We have there a heap of worthy people, little *rentiers*, dealers in ginghams and prints, grocers, and pastry-cooks, who are now the owners of acres, but haven't the least idea what to do with them, not having the smallest notion of agricultural methods.

I don't see any one but his Excellency who really knows what he's about. This extraordinary man knows everything, has seen everything, read everything, and there is something wonderful in the vividness with which he conceives. Unfortunately he can't be everywhere at once; and then he is too kind, too unable to believe any harm. Thus he still clings to his faith in the Belgian, that scoundrel and swindler and liar; he still expects to see him arrive with fresh hands and provisions, so that every day when I go into his room his first word is, "No ship in sight this morning, Pascalon?"

And to think that so humane a man, so excellent a ruler, already has enemies! Yes, he has enemies. There are ill-disposed people in the city. He knows it; he smiles at it; he says to me: "What will you have, my child? I'm the 'state of things,' and there are always people who are against the 'state of things.'"

October 8th.—Spent the morning in taking the census of our little colony. This document on the early phases of a little State which will perhaps become a great one, has the curious feature of having been drawn up by one of the founders, one of those who helped to break ground.

October 10th.—Water, water, nothing but

water. In these floods of damp, this continual drenching, one grows wofully slack, loses all taste for anything, turns sour and ill-natured, universally disgusted, quite as when one has been taking bromide.

A party of the disaffected is forming in the city, with Costecalde for chief and ringleader. They assemble at the place they call the Café Pinus, which consists of two or three tables and a couple of benches in one of the cubicles. It appears to exist for the purpose of drinking bottled lemonade. Pinus, in the whole colony, is the only man who is making any money, and he makes it by the sale of this fizzing liquid.

These gatherings under his roof have been kept up very late, and have filled the big house with such a clatter of discussion that complaints have been made in the city. The racket keeps the children awake. Therefore the Governor has been obliged to give orders for the closing of the establishment—a measure that has produced a bad effect on many minds.

It so happens that another affair has contributed to the state of tension. The Marquis des Espazettes and a few other crack shots, kept in-doors by the dreadful rain, lately conceived the idea of setting up targets formed of old tin boxes, disused receptacles of sweetmeats and tunny, of sardines and potted pears, and then of firing at them the livelong day from the windows.

Our former cap-shooters, now that helmets and caps are not so easy to replace, have thus been converted into can-shooters.

In itself this is not a bad exercise, but Costecalde has succeeded in persuading the Governor that it leads to a deplorable waste of powder.

Out comes, therefore, a new decree, prohibiting this expensive sport. The can-shooters are furious, the aristocracy sulks. This was precisely what Costecalde had foreseen. Oh, he's up to snuff!

But, after all, what can you bring against our poor Governor? The d——d Dutchman has let him in, just as he has let us all in. But is it his fault if it keeps on raining, and if the bad weather prevents us from getting forward with the bull-baiting? Our national sport, you know, was promised us from the first; but up to this time it has been impossible to set it going.

There has been a kind of blight on this familiar pastime. Our good Tarasconians, who had been cut off from it in France, rejoiced in the thought of giving it a new life here. We brought with us expressly some cows, and a bull of the Camargue—Old Roman—the same who used to win such fame on our votive anniversaries.

On account of the rains, which have rendered it impossible to leave them at pasture, these beasts have been kept in a stable; but all of a sudden, without any one's knowing in the least how it happened—I shouldn't be surprised if

Costecalde had had a hand in this too Old Roman has got out.

Now he's roaming the forest, he has become wild, he's no longer a bull—he's a buffalo.

Of course we've tried to catch him again, but he's quite too terrible. In reality he's baiting us, instead of our baiting him. And he's the only wild animal in the colony!

I wonder if this, too, is Tartarin's fault?

Ah, things are going wrong. Heaven watch over our Governor!

II.

Day after day, page after page, through strokes as fine as the gray slant of the rain, with the desperate dead monotony of the watery, watery waste, we content ourselves with giving the sense, though with scrupulous fidelity, of our friend Pascalon's diary.

As the intercourse between the town and headquarters continued to be characterized by a visible tension, Tartarin, to recover a measure of popularity, determined at last to organize the bull-baiting; not, of course, with the assistance of Old Roman, who was still ranging the thicket, constantly wilder and more of a buffalo, but with that of the three cows which remained.

Very attenuated, very lean, and sad to behold were these domestic animals of our country, accustomed to the open air and the sun, and immured ever since their arrival at Port Tarascon in a damp, dark stable. Never mind, this was better than nothing.

On the sandy shore, beside the sea, the spot forming the usual parade-ground of the militia, a platform had been erected in advance, and a circus enclosed by ropes, according to the custom in Provence.

Advantage was taken of a glimpse of fine weather, a day when the sun almost shone, and

the Governor, the high dignitaries, and their ladies assumed their places on the platform. All costumes were displayed—all the bespangled mantles—and the women had extracted their best-preserved finery from the depths of their trunks.

Every one seemed happy, touched with the

intoxication of the game, down to the little ones who ran round and round the ring, pursuing each other with cries of "There! there! the cattle!" while the higher personages settled themselves in their rows, and the underlings and militiamen, with their wives and daughters and maid-servants, pressed together round the ropes.

Forgotten at this moment was the weariness of the long rainy days, forgotten were the grievances against the Belgian — the dirty Belgian. "There! there! the cattle!" this cry of the children sufficed to rekindle the good-humor of the mobile race who are cheered up by a sunbeam. "There! there! the cattle!" Yes, at Port Tarascon we could have our bull-baiting: different enough from what it had come to be in the old country: no one to worry the poor plain folk, to deprive them of their favorite pleasure.

And what folly, indeed, ever to have forbidden the bull-baiting of our gentle southern France, in which there is nothing bloody, nothing cruel; in which it is only a question of plucking off a cockade planted between the horns of a bull! Doubtless the sport is not absolutely harmless. It requires skill and agility. But, on the whole, accidents are rare, and are reducible to a few innocuous bruises.

The flourish of trumpets, under the direction of Escourbaniès, Chief of the Levies and the Orpheon, mingled its brazen uproar with the cries and the rumble of the crowd. After the "Port Tarascon March" had been played several times, the drums beat a loud tattoo.

It was the signal. The circus, which had suddenly become a field of danger, emptied itself in a trice, and one of the animals entered the lists, greeted with frantic hurrahs.

She had nothing very terrible about her, the poor scared cow, with her ribs showing through, who stared at the crowd from big eyes disaccustomed to the light of heaven; she only began to "mooh," and stood still, sticking fast in the middle of the arena, with her big tricolored cockade between her horns.

One of the baiters came and "shaved" her, as the term is, passing behind and before her, clapping his hands and trying to excite her. "There! there! there!" But she suffered him to approach her, even to touch her, and remained quite peaceful and resigned, without the slightest disposition to retaliate. There would have been neither peril nor honor in relieving her of her cockade.

At this sight the public got indignant, and cried for the irons—the irons! Then two men came forward, armed with long poles tipped with irons in the shape of tridents. When they pricked the poor thing's nose, instead of losing her temper, as usual, she uttered a plaintive low and fled, rushing round the course, pursued, belabored, with all the world at her heels, in the midst of hisses and hootings and shouts. "Enough! enough!" cried the crowd. "Zou! zou! put her out! put her out." She retired in extreme humiliation.

The second cow absolutely refused to leave the stable. Neither shouts nor blows nor proddings could overcome her reluctance. It was vain to push her; it was fruitless to pull her; it was impossible to drag her across the threshold.

So they gave their attention to the third, who was said to be very vicious with her blood up. She entered the circus on the gallop, digging her forked hoofs into the sand, lashing her sides with her tail, and butting vigorously right and left. The inquiring spectators who had lingered in the arena skipped nimbly out of her way, clearing the course on the spot.

This time, at least, there would be a fine game. Not much, however, as it turned out. The animal dashed away, bounded over the rope, cleaving the crowd, taking aim with her horns, and rushing straight to the sea, hurled herself into it.

With water up to the hock, then up to the shoulder, she went out as far as she could go. Soon nothing more of her was seen than her poor nose above the water, where her two horns formed a crescent, with the cockade in the middle. She remained there till evening, wofully lowing; and the whole settlement, from the shore, called her names, hissed her, and assailed her with stones, hootings, and gibes, of which last missiles the poor "state of things," who had come down from his platform, had also quite his share.

The collapse of the national game was a great check to the Government, of which the disaffected party made haste to take advantage. "Monkey's work—little of it, and that little bad," said

the bilious Costecalde, with his wicked grin. This was the way he spoke of all the Governor's acts.

Something at any rate had to be done to drain off so much fermentation. The Government therefore conceived the idea of an expedition against King Nagonko. The scoundrel had fled from the island, with his Papuans, after the death of the unfortunate Bravida, and nothing had been heard of him since. It was said that he inhabited a neighboring island six or eight miles away, whose vague outline was distinguishable on clear days, but invisible most of the time, thanks to the continual rains and the curtain of fog.

The unavenged insult to the Tarasconian flag was one of the greatest grievances of Costecalde's section, one of his most powerful arguments against the "state of things." These were pointed mainly at the cowardice of the head of affairs, who had exacted no reparation for the death of the unhappy Bravida, none for that of Cambalalette or of Father Vezole, to say nothing of so many other compatriots devoured by the savages.

In the *entourage* of Tartarin there had been much talk of some really great attempt. Brother Bataillet preached war as he alone could preach it. Tartarin himself, with all that was pacific in him, had long resisted. But so many ill-natured remarks were retailed to him that at last his patience broke down. As we say at Tarascon, "Little flies make big donkeys jump." He therefore took a great decision, hoping thus to re-establish his popularity, and the expedition was prepared.

When the long-boat had been put into condition, repaired and provisioned, and the culverin, handled by Brother Bataillet and Galoffre the verger, set up in the prow, twenty militia-men, all well armed, went aboard under the orders of Escourbaniès and the Marquis des Espazettes, and one morning they set sail.

Their absence was to last three days, and these three days seemed extremely long to the colony. What would be the result of so adventurous a cruise? To what dangers would the expedition not be exposed? Would it come back at all? These anxieties were fostered by the perfidious machinations of Costecalde, who kept gnawing like a wood-louse at his rival's reputation, and went about saying, "What an imprudence! as if it would not have been much better to leave the wretches alone!"

Towards the end of the third day the report of a cannon, rolling over the deep, brought down the whole population to the shore, from which the long-boat was seen to approach at a rapid pace, under all her sail, with her nose in the air, as if borne on a breeze of triumph.

Even before she had reached the strand the joyous cries of her company—the "Let's make a noise!" of Escourbaniès—announced from afar the complete success of the enterprise.

An exemplary vengeance had been extorted from the cannibals, heaps of villages had been burned, and, according to every one's account, thousands of Papuans slain.

The figure varied, but was always enormous, and the accounts were rather different too. In

any case, what was certain was that they had five or six prisoners of mark to show, among whom were King Nagonko himself and his daughter Likiriki.

The prisoners were conducted to headquarters amid the ovations rendered by the crowd to the victors. The soldiers filed out in great array, carrying, like the companions of Columbus on his return from the discovery of the New World, all sorts of strange objects—brilliant plumes, skins of beasts, weapons, and spoils of the savages.

But the prisoners were especially surrounded as they passed, the good Tarasconians examining them with all the curiosity of hate. Brother Bataillet had caused a few draperies, which they ineffectually held together, to be thrown over their black bareness; and to see them thus figged out, to say to one's self that they had eaten up Father Vezole, Notary Cambalalette, and so many others, gave one the same shudder of repulsion that one feels in menageries, in the presence of anacondas digesting under dirty blankets.

King Nagonko marched first—an old blackamoor with a big belly, and a mass of crinkled white wool that sat on his head like a smoking-cap. A red clay pipe—the kind they make at Marseilles—was attached to his left arm by a bit of string. Near him came the little Likiriki, with shining, impish eyes, bedecked with coral necklaces and bracelets of pink shells. They were followed by the others, great monkeys with long arms, who showed their pointed teeth in the grimace of their horrible smiles.

There were a few jokes about them at first, such as that they would give Mademoiselle Tournatoire plenty of work, and the good old

spinster, revisited by her famous fixed idea, began indeed to think how she could turn them out; but curiosity was quickly converted to fury as we remembered the fate of our baked and boiled compatriots.

Presently many people began to cry "Death! death to them all! Zou! zou!" To give himself a more military stamp, Escourbaniès had adopted Scrapouchinat's phrase, and kept crying that we must have them all shot like green monkeys.

Tartarin turned towards him and checked his ravings with a gesture. "Spiridion," he said, "let us respect the laws of war."

But moderate your ecstasy. Tartarin had his plan.

A consistent defender of our old friend the duke, if he had never given in to his being an impostor, he had yet at bottom had his suspicions. If, after all, one had been taken in by a vulgar swindler, the treaty for the purchase of the island, which his Grace pretended to have made with Nagonko, would then be as false as all the rest; the island would not be ours, and our vouchers for the acres, our great bargains, would be nothing but so much waste paper.

Accordingly, as soon as the prisoners had been introduced into the citadel, the Governor, far from thinking of shooting them like green monkeys, offered the Papuan monarch a solemn reception.

This was just the sort of thing he knew how to do, deeply versed in everything that had been done by Captain Cook, by Bougainville, and other great navigators.

He simply approached the dusky monarch and began to rub noses with him.

The barbarian seemed extremely surprised, as in his tribe this fashion had been long abandoned, had become quite a lost tradition.

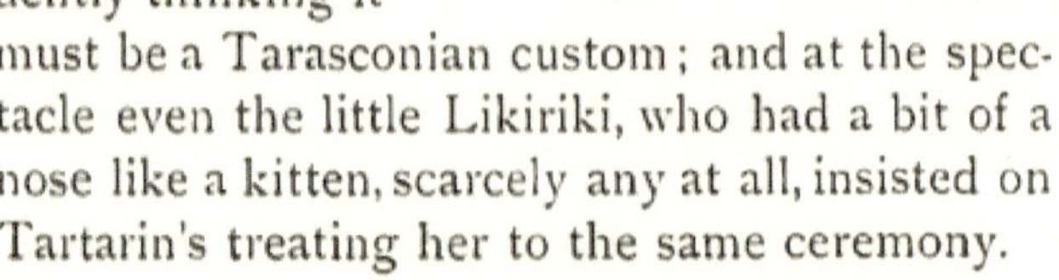

He submitted none the less, evidently thinking it must be a Tarasconian custom; and at the spectacle even the little Likiriki, who had a bit of a nose like a kitten, scarcely any at all, insisted on Tartarin's treating her to the same ceremony.

When the rubbing of noses was over, arose the question of communicating verbally with the brutes.

Brother Bataillet spoke to them first, in his Papuan of the other side; but naturally, as it was not the Papuan of this side, they couldn't understand. Cicero Franquebalme, who knew English after a fashion, tried them with the idiom of Shakespeare. Escourbaniès mumbled out a few words of Spanish, but without more success than the others.

"Let us, at any rate, give them something to eat," said Tartarin.

So a few boxes of tunny were opened. This time the savages understood, and threw themselves upon the dainties in question, while the Governor and Commissioners surrounded them, watching them gluttonously devour and empty the boxes, scraping them to the bottom with fingers dripping with oil. Then, after several great swigs of brandy, which they seemed particularly to appreciate, the King, to the general's stupefaction, began to troll out in a hoarse voice our Tarasconian revolutionary song about chucking the refractory from the big window. Hiccoughed forth by this thick-lipped barbarian, with his mouth smeared with red and his teeth with black, it had a fantastic, ferocious sound.

So, then, Nagonko knew our local language.

After a minute of amazement the anomaly was explained.

During the few months of association with the hapless passengers of the *Farandole* and the

Lucifer, the Papuans had picked up a certain amount of Tarasconian—a Tarasconian of no great elegance, no doubt, and consisting mainly of the expressions of the Rabblebabble; but

with the aid of gestures it helped to enable our friends to communicate with them.

So they communicated.

Questioned on the subject of our ally the duke, Nagonko declared that he had never, never in his life, heard of this distinguished personage, or of any one who remotely resembled him.

The island had never been sold.

There had never been any treaty.

Never any treaty? Tartarin, on the spot, caused one to be drawn up. The scholarly Franquebalme had an extensive hand in the framing of this severe and scrupulous document. He availed himself in it of all his legal erudition—whatsoever, whensoever, and wheresoever at every step—so that, with its Roman cement, the thing made a compact and solid whole.

Nagonko ceded the island in exchange for a barrel of rum, ten pounds of tobacco, two cotton umbrellas, and a dozen dog-collars.

A career of usefulness was thus opened to these last objects of traffic, which had been brought in such quantities because Tartarin had read in the works of travellers that they are particularly appreciated by the savages of Oceanica.

A codicil affixed to the treaty authorized

Nagonko, his daughter, and his companions to reside on the west coast of the island, the direction in which the settlers never trusted themselves, for fear of Old Roman, the famous bull who had become a buffalo.

The business was concluded in secret session —knocked off in a few hours.

In this manner, thanks to their great leader's diplomatic ability, the bonds and vouchers of the colonists became valid again, really representing something.

And who was taken in this time? That plotter of a Costecalde and his partisans.

Who, on the other hand, was very happy? The author of the *Memorial*, Pascalon, the gentle stutterer, now more than ever in love with his mum-mum-master.

III.

MEANWHILE we continued to be drenched, for out of the continual grayness the water continued to fall. Lord, how it fell! In the morning, when the windows of the big house were opened on a crack, inquiring hands were thrust out.

"Is it raining?"

"It *is* raining!"

"Another day of it?"

"Another day of it!"

Yes; it rained as it had rained in Bézuquet's account of it.

Poor Bézuquet! In spite of all the misery he had endured with his mates of the *Farandole* and the *Lucifer*, he had staid over at Port Tarascon, not daring to return in his tattooed condition to any Christian land. Resuming the attributes of an apothecary—he was now a simple medical assistant, very low in rank, under the orders of Tournatoire—the late Provisional

Governor preferred exile, even in these conditions, to the exhibition in civilized countries of his monstrous countenance and his hands all pricked with vermilion.

To avenge himself for his misfortune, he made the most grewsome predictions to the others. If they complained of the rain, of the mud, of the mildew, he shrugged his shoulders.

"Oh, just wait a bit, my dears; there's better still to come."

And Bézuquet was not mistaken. Living, as you might say, half in the water, with no fresh meat to eat, many of us began to pay for it.

The cows had long since been eaten up, condemned immediately after our fruitless attempt to make them figure in the arena. Only one of them was reserved, in case of symptoms of famine. The settlement had ceased to look to its hunters, though there were such crack shots among them, all penetrated with Tartarin's principles, counting three times for a quail and twice for a partridge. The bother was that there were neither partridges nor quails, nor anything that resembled them, neither the gull nor the sea-mew, nor any other bird of the ocean ever touching at this side of the island. All that the hunters encountered in their excursions were a few wild pigs — very few indeed --and here and there a kangaroo, who was very difficult to hit on account of its leaps and bounds.

With this animal Tartarin was rather at a

loss to say how much to count. One day, when the great shot, the marquis, questioned him on the subject, he replied, a little at a venture, "I think your lordship had better count six."

His lordship counted six, but brought home from his ducking nothing but a very bad and very incurable cold.

"I see that I shall have to go myself," said Tartarin; but he kept putting off this excursion, and game kept growing constantly scarcer. Certainly the big lizards were not bad, but if you ate nothing else you grew terribly tired of their tasteless white flesh. Bouffartigue, the pastry-cook, adapting a receipt of our clever monks at home, had found a way of potting and preserving it, but in the long-run the colony got very sick of it.

The want of exercise completed the effect of the absence of fresh meat. Nobody went out; everybody stayed moping in the big house. What in the world should they have done outside, lackaday! in the rain, in the great pools, in the lake of mud that surrounded them?

There was not much "walking round" in the evening. A few of the pluckier ones — Escarras, Dourladoure, Mainfort, Roquetaillade — sometimes started, in spite of the downpour, to have a dig at the ground, to try and do something with their acres, loath to give up all attempt to plant. But they came back aching with pleurisy and pneumonia, or else their sowing produced the most extraordinary things. In the hot humidity of the drenched earth a celery-stalk would become in a night a gigantic tree, hard enough to crack your teeth. That sort of thing couldn't be eaten. The development of the cabbage was phenomenal, but it was all in stem as long as an alpenstock. As for potatoes and carrots, they were no use at all.

Bézuquet had told the truth when he said that things would either not come up at all or come up too far.

To these manifold causes of demoralization add the simple disease of "pining," of home-sickness, a longing for sun-warmed nooks and corners, under old walls gilded with the light of Provence; for our great, fresh, healthy breezes, when the mistral bends the rows of cypresses, or splits off in great scales the bark of the plane-tree.

Nothing of that sort on the wretched island —nothing but permanent rain. The number of the sick couldn't fail to increase steadily. Happily for them the Commissioner of Health, more of a Tarasconian than of a doctor, had a limited faith in the pharmacopœia.

"I'm not one of your druggers and dosers," he said. Just the opposite in this of his predecessor, Bézuquet.

Every morning, on their rounds, this pair met at the bedsides of their patients, and while Bézuquet instantly suggested his various poultices and plasters, Tournatoire only prescribed a nice little garlic broth.

And it is not to be denied, my fine friend, as they say down there, you had people all swelled up, without voice or breath, already wanting to save their souls and make their wills, when in came the nice little garlic broth, three sprigs for a small pot, a bit of roast meat in three spoonfuls of olive oil, and the same individuals who had been so far gone began to sniff and say, "Bless my soul, it smells good!"

The mere smell immediately brought them round.

They took a plate, then another plate, and at the third they were sitting up, sir, or even standing up, with their voices restored and the swelling quite gone down. In the evening you saw them in the parlor taking a hand at bézique. Ah! the garlic of salvation, the garlic of Providence!

A single patient, a patient of position, the high and mighty lady, Madame des Espazettes de Lambesc, had rejected Tournatoire's remedy. Garlic broth was good for the Rabblebabble, but when one comes down from the Crusades— She wouldn't hear of it any more than she would hear of the marriage of her daughter Clorinde to Pascalon. As soon as either this marriage or the garlic broth was mentioned, she gave a "Pouah!" of haughty disgust, which, in the Tarasconian fashion, she pronounced "Puai!"

The unhappy lady was, however, in a very bad way. Yes, poor thing, she had got it. Understand by this vague pronoun the inscrutable, preposterous, aqueous ailment which had settled upon our little band of Southrons. Those whom it attacked suddenly became very ugly, their eyes began to goggle, their arms and legs to swell; it made them think of the terrible disease let loose by Mr. Mauve in the legend of the Son of Man.

The poor marquise had begun to "protrude" everywhere. I beg your pardon for this peculiar expression. It occurs in the *Memorial* amid the record, full of delicate emotion, of our gentle and desperate Pascalon's visits to the city.

Authorized to pay them without hope, he turned up at the big house every evening and found the marquise in bed, under the shelter of a great blue cotton umbrella attached to the head of her couch. This arrangement prevailed in all the cubicles, on account of the cracks in the roof and the sudden leaks from conduits that had burst.

But while she kept groaning under her umbrella, the marquise would have nothing to do with the garlic broth. To the entreaties of her husband, of her daughter, even of Pascalon, who sometimes ventured to propose, with his stutter, a little sou-sou-soup, she replied, with an inexpressible gesture of disgust, "Puai!"

Then the unfortunate Pascalon remained silent, seated near the bed, watching the noble lady "protrude" still further; while the long Clorinde, preparing the camomile tea, came and went with the graceful skip of a young kangaroo, and the marquis, in a corner, philosophically filled his cartridges for the next day's chase.

Roundabout in the neighboring cubicles the water trickled down on the open umbrellas, the children squalled, and contentious sounds, the uproar of political discussion, came in from the saloon, mingled with the perpetual patter of the rain on the windows, on the zinc patch of the roof, and the universal guttering of the water.

Between whiles Costecalde kept up his underhand intrigues, by day at headquarters, and in the evening in the private room that had been assigned to him as Commissioner of Agriculture. Barban and Rugimabaud, who had sold their souls to him, helped him to diffuse the most sinister rumors, this one among others, "The garlic is giving out!"

It was appalling to think that it *might* run short in the government emporium, this blessed garlic, the savior, the healer, the universal panacea. Costecalde accused the "state of things" of monopolizing it for himself and his creatures —of committing personal excesses with it.

Escourbaniès (and with what a voice!) backed up these calumnies of his brother Commissioner. There is a Tarasconian proverb which says that the scoundrels who quarrel by day steal together at night. This was quite the case with the double-faced Escourbaniès, who at headquarters, before Tartarin, talked against Costecalde, while in town in the evening he took (what will you have?) the opposite line; obeying thus an instinct of flattery which always led him, such was his desire to please, to grovel before the person with whom he happened to find himself.

The women took part in these discussions, and they were not the least contentious debaters; their tongues went like windmills; they made more noise than all the men together, including Escourbaniès. Indeed, this political interference of the ladies was one of the greatest dangers for the party in power; for though in our southern households the woman is not supposed to count for much, and has not the formal honors, she is in reality the pivot of the family life.

Tartarin, whose kindness and patience we have not now to discover, bore up long against these manœuvres.

He was far, indeed, from being unaware of them. In the evening, when he smoked his pipe, leaning on his elbows at his open window—for, in spite of the rain, his powerful nature needed the refreshment of the outer air—while he listened in this attitude to all the sounds of the night, the murmur of the Little Rhone mixed with those of all the rivulets formed by the downpour on the hills, he distinguished distant voices, the echoes of speeches, and saw through the thick atmosphere (it was as thick as water could make it) the wavering lights in the casements of the big house. Political passions surged and sputtered yonder in the city.

The heart of our great Tartarin bled at the thought that all this confusion was caused by that monster of a Costecalde; his hand trembled on the window-bar, his eye darted a flame in the dusk—he could fancy himself on the track of a wild beast. But as, after all, these emotions, combined with the damp of the night, might bring on the disease, he controlled himself, closed the window again, and went quietly to bed.

At last, however, matters reached such a point that he decided on a great step.

He suspended the pay of Costecalde and his two myrmidons; he abrogated their titles and dignities, and even deprived the first-named of his mantle of Grandee of the First Class. He appointed Beaumevieille, a former haberdasher, Commissioner—a very honest man, though not perhaps knowing much more about planting and reaping than his predecessor. Beaumevieille would, at any rate, be admirably seconded by Labranque, a former manufacturer of oil-cloth, and Rébuffat—the one who used to keep the great place for caramels; they were to replace Rugimabaud and Barban as sub-commissioners.

The Governor's decree was posted up early in town, that is to say, on the door of the big house; so that Costecalde, coming out in the morning to proceed to his office, received the affront of it full in his face. Which was a mighty good job, adds Pascalon in his *Memorial*.

This *coup d'ètât* produced an immense agitation in the settlement. The settlers flew about, reading the decree over and over and criticising it, so that the general residence had the buzz of a frightened hive.

For a long time back Costecalde and his minions had held themselves ready for a movement, and it may be seen by what followed how right Tartarin was to act with vigor.

Lord save us, it was only just time!

In the space of four or five hours some twenty, perhaps, of the disaffected sprang up and directed their steps to the citadel; these comprised the former habitués of the Café Pinus, together with Pinus himself, who had never forgiven the closing of his establishment. They were all armed to the teeth, and they all cried: "Down with the Governor! Death to the Governor! Chuck him into the Rhone! Zou, zou! Resignation! Resignation!"

The troop was followed by four or five excited viragoes, and by the precious Escourbaniès, howling even louder than the others:

"Resign! Resign! Let's make a noise—make a noise!"

Unfortunately it was raining, it was pouring, and this obliged each of them to hold his umbrella in one hand and his gun in the other.

Besides, the Government had taken its measures.

Passing the Little Rhone, the insurgents found themselves before the citadel, and what did they see there?

On the first floor Tartarin loomed up at the window, armed with his deadly Winchester and supported by his faithful cap-shooters and can-shooters, the infallible marquis much to the fore; all of them shots, mind you, who, at twenty paces, counting four, could put their ball into the little round label on a box of potted pears.

But what frightened the wretches above all was the appearance of Brother Bataillet, who, under the hood of the great door, bent over his culverin, ready to fire at the first sign from Tartarin.

So terrible and unexpected was the sight of this artillery and its lighted match that the rebels wavered, and Escourbaniès, turning one of the moral somersaults which he so frequently practised, had time to begin to dance the horn-pipe of success under Tartarin's window, roaring out, as fast as he could draw breath: "Long live the Governor! Long live the 'state of things!' Let's make a noise! Ah! ah! ah!"

Tartarin, from his lofty post, still handling his thirty-two shooter, responded, in a ringing voice: "Let's turn in again, my disaffected friends. The rain is coming down, and I am loath to expose you longer to such inconvenience. We shall now call together our good subjects in their *comitia*, and inquire of the nation if our services be any longer required. I recommend quiet until then—or else just step back!"

The vote was taken on the morrow, and the actual state of things re-elected by a crushing majority.

A few days later, as a contrast to all this agitation, occurred a touching ceremony, the christening of young Likiriki, the little Papuan princess, daughter of King Nagonko and pupil of Brother Bataillet. His Reverence had completed the work of conversion inaugurated by Father Vezole—God be praised!

She was truly a delightful little monkey, this yellow-skinned princess, bedecked with red necklaces, in the short frock striped with blue made for her by Mademoiselle Tournatoire. Buoyant, elastic, plump, and round, she could never keep still—her legs were perpetually going off like a clown's.

The Governor was godfather, and Madame Franquebalme godmother. She was christened under the names of Mary-Martha-Tartarina. Only, on account of the dreadful weather that prevailed that day, as it prevailed the day before, and as it would prevail on the morrow, the function could not take place, as in the case of Miraclete, at St. Martha's of the Palms, which was now half full of water, its roof of foliage having long since fallen in.

The company collected for the ceremony in the saloon of the general residence, but this did not prevent our dreamy and poetic Pascalon from harking back to the happy day on which he too had stood at the font with his dear Clorinde, so often denied him, yet so consistently loved.

The passage in his diary—we continue simply to give the general drift of it—bearing on this episode is marked with a trace of tears, almost blurring out the words, "Poor little me and poor little she!"

It was on the day following the baptism of Likiriki-Tartarina that a most frightful catastrophe occurred. But the facts here acquire a gravity; let us leave the story to the *Memorial.*

IV.

December 4th.—To-day, the second Sunday in Advent, we have been visited by a fearful calamity, of which the consequences are deplorable, and the effect on the settlement may be most disastrous.

The verger Galoffré, Inspector of the Navy, on going to examine the long-boat, as he does every morning, finds it gone.

The staple, the chain, the whole fastening have been pulled out.

He thought at first it might be some new trick of Nagonko and his gang, as we are always suspicious of them; he thought that during the night they might have been prowling about this side of the island.

But, lo and behold, in the cavity left in the post by the extraction of the staple, the Inspector discovered, quite soaked with water and soiled with mud, an envelope addressed to his Excellency!

Guess, now, what this envelope contained.

A visiting-card of our gracious Costecalde, still inscribed with all his titles, Commissioner of Agriculture and Grandee of the First Class, and bearing in the corner, in pencil, the letters P. P. C. Beneath were the names of Barban and Rugimabaud, together with those of four militiamen, Caissargue, Bouillargue, Truphénus, and Roquetaillade.

For some days past the launch had been quite ready, supplied with provisions in view of a new expedition planned by his doughty Reverence.

The wretches took advantage of this piece of good-luck. They have carried off the whole blessed thing, even the compass and their very muskets.

Oh, the brigands! oh, the deserters!—to call them thieves is to flatter them!

And to think that the first three are married—that they leave behind them their wives and a litter of brats! Their wives I can understand—at a pinch you may leave your wife—but the children are another matter.

In the city, at first, the thing was not believed; but after no room was left for doubt, you should have seen the general uprising against the traitors!

Madame Costecalde, a poor affair, reduced to idiocy by her husband, was completely crushed. The two others, Madame Barban and Madame Rugimabaud, veritable furies, called down on the heads of their respective ruffians every conceivable catastrophe—shipwreck and drowning, with some barbarian belly for a tomb. Madame Barban especially yelled out her imprecations, her hands trembling with rage like the twigs of a tree.

The general feeling evoked by this event has been a kind of stupor. It seems now as if our communications with the rest of the world were destroyed. So long as we had the launch there remained some hope of our reaching the continent by a kind of progress from island to island—some belief in the possibility of looking for help.

Brother Bataillet broke into a terrible rage, appealing to heaven for all its thunder-bolts against our wrongers. Escourbaniès, characteristically, went about shouting that we ought to have them shot like green monkeys, and that by way of reprisals we ought to put their wives and children to the sword.

The Governor alone kept his equilibrium.

"We must not get started," he remarked to Escourbaniès. "After all, they are still Tarasconians. Let us pity them; let us think of the dangers they must run. Truphénus alone among them has some idea of the management of a sail."

Then came to him the fine thought of making the forsaken children the wards of the colony.

At bottom, I suspect he was not sorry to have got rid of his mortal enemy and the latter's minions.

During the day his Excellency dictated me the following general order, which has been posted up in town:

"General Order.

"We, Tartarin of Tarascon, Governor of Port Tarascon and its Dependencies, Grand Ribbon of the Order, etc., etc., etc.,

"Recommend to the population the greatest calm.

"The guilty parties will be followed up with energy, and subjected to all the rigor of the law.

"The Commissioner of Artillery and of the Navy is charged with the execution of the present order."

Then, to wind up, and to reply to certain evil rumors that have been for some time in circulation, he directed me to add this postscript:

"The garlic will not give out."

December 6th.—The Governor's order has produced the very best effect in the city.

A reflection might, indeed, have been made as to how we shall follow them up, and in what direction, and with what means of getting afloat, inasmuch as we have no idea where they have gone, and no boat into the bargain. But it is not for nothing that one of our local proverbs says that you must take man by his tongue and the bull by his horns. The Tarasconian race is so sensitive to fine words, letting them lead it so by the nose, that no one has doubted or questioned for a moment.

Moreover, a sunbeam happened to peep out between two showers, and this was enough to cheer every one up. Now, for the hour, we all turn out on the Walk Round; we do nothing but laugh and lark. Ah, the good old stock—the dear old stock!

December 10th.—An unheard-of honor has befallen me. I have been created Grandee of the First Class.

At breakfast this morning I found my patent under my plate. The Governor shows himself delighted to have been able to confer on me this high distinction. Franquebalme, Baumevieille, and Brother Bataillet seem equally gratified with myself at this new dignity which renders me their equal.

It has rained, of course, but to-day the rain has struck me, somehow, as less dreary.

In the evening, my visit to the city. The news was already known, and among my noble friends I was particularly congratulated. The marquis gave me the accolade, Clorinde was flushed with pleasure. No one but her ladyship appeared indifferent to my happiness.

Still awfully sick, still declining to have anything to do with the garlic broth, she struck me, under her umbrella, as protruding and sulking still more. Haughty as ever, she referred with contempt to my wonderful investiture—"Puai!" In her eyes, even this does not elevate me in the social scale. Dear me, what in the world does she want? To come in for the first class—at my age!

But, in spite of everything, I cherish the

hope that this new dignity, the honors with which I am overwhelmed, the importance of my functions, and the brilliancy of my future, will, perhaps, finally get the better of her feeling of caste.

December 10th.—A dreadful rumor—in a whisper—is going the rounds: the garlic *is* running down!

If it should really give out, what on earth would be the end of us?

Frightful, indeed, to have to face without garlic the innumerable feverish forms of rheumatism that besiege us!

December 14th.—Something extraordinary is going on at headquarters—something so extraordinary that I scarcely dare to hint at it in this record. I have doubted long of so strange an anomaly, but at last it has become visible for all—so visible that last evening, in town, all the world was talking of it.

The Governor entertains a feeling!

And for whom, pray? Why, for the little monkey Likiriki, his godchild, who is certainly a nice little thing, but has none the less remained, under her varnish of education and conversion, a lying, pilfering, gluttonous, dangerous savage.

He—*he!* Tartarin, our great Tartarin, who

might have made the grandest matches, practically in love with a monkey! Royal blood, if you will, but with manners and customs so grotesque, with her little skirt in rags, and her little

person, on the days it doesn't rain, perched on the top of some cocoanut-tree, from which she amuses herself with dropping fruits as big as rocks on the heads of our most venerable settlers. The other day she almost put an end to one of the fathers of the state.

If any one asks where her Highness may be, you hear something scramble down from the branches, and the young lady presents herself. And then, what manners at home!

I needn't call attention to their disparity of age. Tartarin is quite sixty, grizzled, and finely filled out, whereas she is only twelve or fourteen at the most—with these creatures you can never tell.

I had certainly noticed sundry indications, but I couldn't attach importance to them. For instance, the indulgence of the Governor to the old villain Nagonko—his allowances and attentions—always keeping him to dinner when he comes to headquarters. You should see the filthy ways of the old gorilla—how he eats with his fingers, and stuffs himself with everything, especially with brandy.

He always ends with his incongruous song, in his still more incongruous Provençal, about chucking people out of the window. In short, no sort of form.

Tartarin has always treated all this as his cheery, cordial ways; and whenever the little princess, following her father's example, has played some trick that has given us all a shiver in the back, the good Governor has only smiled, beaming on her with paternal looks that seem to make excuses for her, and to remind us that she is only a child.

And, indeed, in spite of these symptoms, and others still more conclusive, I continue to doubt.

December 18th.—Impossible to doubt any longer.

This morning in council the Governor opened on the subject of his marriage to the little princess.

He put forward the ground of policy, talked of a *mariage de convenance*, of the interests of the settlement. He dwelt on the relations of our little state, without alliances, lost on the bosom of the deep. By marrying the daughter of a Papuan king he would secure us a fleet of pirogues, an army of mercenaries.

No one in the council raised an objection.

Escourbaniès the first, dashed forward, stamping with enthusiasm: "Perfect, your Excellency—a capital idea! Ah! ah! ah! When may we look for the wedding?" This evening, in town, who knows what infamies he will have invented?

Cicero Franquebalme by force of habit sorted into two interminable little heaps, on the one side and on the other, the arguments for and against: "If, on the one hand, the colony, it is not to be denied that on the other," etc., etc. Finally, having considered everything, he gave his assent to the Governor's plan.

Beaumevieille and Tournatoire were of the same opinion; as for Brother Bataillet, he didn't strike me as very warm, but having probably been indoctrinated in advance, he didn't protest.

The funny part of it was the shameless way we all made believe—made believe that it was really a question of the interests of the settlement and of serious alliances. Tartarin, amid a deep approving silence, continued to insist on these high diplomatic considerations.

Then suddenly his kind old eyes filled with bright tears, and he broke out, just as he might have done at home: "And then, do you see, gentlemen, it isn't so much all that—I'm simply fond of the little thing."

This was so simple, so touching, so Tarasconian, that it quite went to our hearts. "Ah, go ahead then, your Excellency, go ahead!" We surrounded him, we pressed his hands. For myself, Pascalon, also in love and having suffered for love, Heaven knows how well I understood him!

December 20th.—The Governor's project is much discussed in town, yet less severely than I should have feared. The men treat it humorously—we are not Tarasconians for nothing—with the drop of mischief that we always mingle with the question of love.

The women are more against him, especially Mademoiselle Tournatoire's little set. Since he wanted to get married, why not take his wife from the nation? Many of them in talking so think, of course, of themselves and their young ladies.

Escourbaniès, coming down to town in the evening, sided quite with the ladies, and put his finger on the weak point of the alliance—the bride's dreadful papa—such a father-in-law! And then to marry a young person who has partaken of our flesh! One couldn't help shuddering.

I felt my blood getting up while the traitor talked, and I bolted out of the room for fear of letting him have my fist in his face. You see our blood is hot at Tarascon.

On leaving the general saloon I called on the Espazettes. The marquise, dreadfully weak, is still in bed, poor woman, determined to be dosed and drugged by Bézuquet rather than give in to Tournatoire and garlic.

In spite of her state, when she saw me come in she began, with haughty raillery, "Well, my Lord Chamberlain, will there be ladies in waiting attached to the new Queen?"

She wanted to make fun of me, but it instantly struck me that there might be an opening in this for Clorinde and me.

Maid of honor or lady in waiting, my beloved would have apartments in the citadel, and I should be able to see her, to speak to her at any hour. Could such happiness be possible?

When I got back the Governor had gone to bed, but I couldn't bear to wait till the morrow to speak to him of my idea. It struck him as sound policy. I lingered late beside his bed, talking over his amours and my own.

December 22d.—Oh, these nobles — race of hawks and vultures!

The marquise won't listen to it.

The marquis at a pinch would make the best of it; with board and lodging at headquarters, better lodging than in town, and sport and garlic at discretion, he would get on very well. But her ladyship—not at any price.

I pause: she's a woman, after all, and I fear my indignation may carry me too far.

December 25th, Christmas Day.—Last night, Christmas Eve, the whole colony assembled in the grand saloon, the Government, the authorities, all the world, and we kept the dear old feast as we might have kept it at home.

Brother Bataillet said midnight mass, and then we hid the fire, as we say in Provence. It is done with a great yule-log, which is carried round the room by the oldest person in the company, and then placed upon the cinders and sprinkled with white wine.

Princess Likiriki was present, laughing immensely, and amused by the ceremony of the log. The special sweets from Montélimar, the Christmas cakes, and all the other delicacies excited her spirits and her appetite.

Then we sang the yule-tide songs that we sing at home: "I saw in the air an angel green," "St. Joseph showed me the Moorish King," and many others.

The songs and the cakes, the great circle round the fire, all brought back the motherland, in spite of the patter of the rain on the roof, and the umbrellas all up on account of the leaks.

At a given moment, whether on purpose or not on purpose, Brother Bataillet struck up on the harmonium the beautiful ballad of our great

poet Mistral—the one about John of Tarascon taken by the pirates.

It is the story of one of our people, who goes among the Turks, assumes the turban, becomes a renegade, and then, when he is on the point of marrying the Sultan's daughter.

hears from the shore an old Tarascon song, sung in the vernacular by mariners from his country.

Then, as the water splashes up under the oar, so a great flood of tears bursts his hard heart. He thinks of the land he has disowned; he thinks and despairs — despairs that he is with the Turks. He pulls off the turban on the spot, flings away the scimitar and the whole business, and goes and joins the little Provençal crew.

At the line about the water splashing up under the oar a general sob broke forth; the Governor himself could scarcely wink away his tears; you saw the grand ribbon of the order go up and down on his athletic chest.

It will, perhaps make a difference in a great many things, this simple ballad of our great Mistral.

December 29th. — To-day, at ten o'clock in the morning, we celebrated the marriage of his Excellency the Governor of Port Tarascon with Princess Royal Likiriki.

The signers of the register were his Majesty the bride's father, who made a cross for his name, the Commissioners, and great dignitaries of the settlement. Mass was said later in the grand saloon.

The ceremony was simple and striking; the troops were all under arms, and every one in full dress. Nagonko alone was rather a blot.

His attitude, both as King and as father, was nothing less than deplorable.

There was nothing to be said against the

princess, who looked very pretty in her white dress, relieved by numerous coral necklaces.

The evening was a great revel, with double rations, salvos of artillery, several rounds from our can-shooters, and acclamations, choruses, and universal joy.

Meanwhile it rains; oh, it does come down!

But the popular rejoicing is not in the least chilled.

V.

"Look! look! A sail! A ship coming in!"

At this cry, uttered one morning by militiaman Berdoulat, who was grubbing for turtles' eggs in the drenching rain, the settlers of Port Tarascon showed themselves at the apertures of their mud-buried ark; and while a thousand cries re-echoed Berdoulat's call, "A sail! Look! look! a sail!" the population, pouring out of windows and doors, frisking and leaping like clowns in a pantomine, rushed down to the beach, which it filled as with the howling of sea-calves.

As soon as the Governor was notified, he also rushed down, and while he went on buttoning, stood radiant under the far from radiant sky, amid the umbrellas of his subjects.

"Well, my children, didn't I tell you he would come at last? It's the duke!"

"The duke?"

"Whom else would you have it be? Certainly, our noble friend, coming to revictual his colony; coming to bring us the weapons and ammunition, the instruments, and those strong arms of the Rabblebabble—bless them! —which I've been asking him for from the first."

You should have seen at this moment the faces of consternation of those who had raved the loudest against the dirty Belgian, for it was not every one who had the impudence of Escourbaniès, and was ready to begin so soon the hornpipe of success. Escourbaniès was already dancing it. "Ah! ah! ah! Long live the Duc de Mons!"

While this went on, a big steamer, high out

of water, very imposing, was moving up the bay. She whistled and let off steam, cast anchor with a great rattle far from the shore, on account of the coral reefs, then remained motionless and silent in the wet.

Our friends began to be rather surprised that the people of the ship were not more eager to return their greeting, and reply to the flapping of their umbrellas and the waving of their hats. They thought his Grace a little cold.

"If it comes to that, perhaps he's not quite sure it's us."

"Perhaps he even knows the way we've been abusing him."

"Abusing him? I never abused him in the world!"

"No more did I; never!"

"No more did I; not a bit!"

Tartarin in all the confusion never lost his head.

He ordered the flag to be flown on the pinnacle of the citadel, and to be backed up by a shot or two.

The shot or two went off, and the Tarasconian colors fluttered in the air.

At the same instant a frightful report resounded through the bay, a cloud of heavy smoke concealed the ship, and a kind of blackbird, passing over the congregated heads with a hoarse hiss, alighted on the roof of the emporium, from which it removed a corner.

At first there was a moment of simple stupor.

"Why, why, they're shoo—shoo—shooting us!" shrieked Pascalon.

Imitating the embodied state, who had given the signal, every one had bounced down on all-fours.

"Dear me, then, it can't be the duke!" said Tartarin, stretched straight on his stomach in the mud.

Near him, wallowing like himself, Franquebalme commenced, in a trembling voice and without changing his position, one of his rigid demonstrations; "If, on the one hand, it were to be the duke, on the other hand there would be reason to suppose—" So he went on.

The arrival of another shell cut his argument short.

Brother Bataillet alone had remained standing. In a thundering voice he called to his gunner, Galoffré, declaring that between them they must reply with the culverin.

"I forbid you to do anything of the sort, if you please!" yelled Tartarin. "Such imprudence! Hold him fast, all of you. Prevent him!"

Torquebiau and Galoffré himself seized his Reverence, each by an arm, and forced him to lie down on his face like the others. At this moment a third shell whizzed over from the ship.

It was plainly to the flag of the colony that these strange missiles were addressed; they were trying to bring down the national colors.

Tartarin grasped the idea, and understood that, if the flag were removed, the shower of shells would probably cease; so he bellowed out, with all the voice he could command: "Devil take it! Haul down the flag!"

Whereupon all the others began to bellow with him: "Haul down the flag! haul down the flag! Don't you hear?"

Every one heard, but nobody hauled, neither settlers, nor soldiers, nor anybody else being eager to climb to such a dangerous eminence. It was the brave maid-servant, to whom they already owed the patching of the roof, who became the heroine of the occasion. She "shinned" up the flag-staff as she was accustomed to "shin," and got possession of the unhappy bunting.

Only then the steamer ceased firing.

A few minutes later two launches laden with soldiers, the glitter of whose arms was perceptible in the distance, put off from the ship, and approached the shore with the steady stroke of the great oars of men-of-war.

As they got nearer, our friends could make out the English colors dragging from the stern in the foamy wake.

The distance was still great, so that Tartarin had time to pick himself up, to tidy himself, and brush off the mud-stains from his clothes —time even to send for the grand ribbon of the order, which he hastily passed over his shoulder.

He looked sufficiently like a public character by the time the two boats ran up the beach.

The first person to jump ashore was an English officer, red-faced and haughty, with his hat cocked up. Behind him came the sailors in a row, with the name of their ship, the *Tomahawk*, on the ribbon of their caps, and these were followed by an escort of marines.

Tartarin, now on his feet and conscious of his grand ribbon, had quite recovered his dignity; he held up his head; his lip curled with the spirit of his great hours.

He waited, having Brother Bataillet on his right and Lawyer Franquebalme on his left.

As for Escourbaniès, instead of remaining with the Governor he had pranced out to meet the English officer, and was quite ready to dance a frantic hornpipe before the victor.

But the representative of her gracious Majesty was not all gracious himself. Without paying the slightest attention to this misplaced bowing and scraping, he turned a somewhat astonished eye over the blue and red umbrellas of the strange tribe before him, and advancing towards Tartarin, inquired in English, "And what nation?"

Franquebalme, understanding a little English, replied: "The Tarasconian."

The officer stared at this announcement of a nationality he had never met with in any chart, and demanded, with still greater insolence: "What are you doing on this island? By what right do you occupy it?"

Franquebalme, deeply disconcerted, translated the inquiry to Tartarin, who exclaimed:

"Answer that the island is ours, Cicero, that it has been ceded to us by King Nagonko, and that we have a treaty in perfect order."

But Franquebalme had no need to go on interpreting. The Englishman turned to the Governor and said, in excellent French:

"King Nagonko? Don't know him!"

At this Tartarin instantly ordered Nagonko to be hunted up and brought down.

While they were waiting, he proposed to the officer to accompany him to headquarters, where the treaty would be exhibited.

The officer assented, and followed Tartarin, leaving a number of his companions in charge of the boats.

The marines were drawn up in a row before them, with their muskets dropped and their bayonets erect—such big, sharp, shiny bayonets!

"Be calm, my children, only be calm," said Tartarin, making his way through the terrified crowd.

The recommendation was very useless except for Brother Bataillet, who continued to foam. But they had their eyes on him; he was narrowly watched. "If your Reverence doesn't mind what he's about, I promise you I'll tie you," said his gunner, wild with terror.

Meanwhile they were looking for Nagonko, and shouting for him everywhere, seemingly in vain. At last a militiaman discovered him hidden among the stores. As the door of the magazine had been smashed in by a shell, he had taken advantage of it to follow up the projectile, and was now snoring between two barrels, drunk with garlic, lamp-oil, and spirits of wine, with our reserve of which he had made terrible havoc.

In this condition, sticky and stinking, dripping with grease, he was brought before the Governor and the English officer. But it was impossible to get a word out of him. He stood there like a log, dumbly glaring.

Then Tartarin had the treaty brought, and read it aloud, showing Nagonko's signature, his cross, and the seals of the Governor and of the grand dignitaries of the colony.

Either this authentic document would prove the settlers' right to the island, or nothing else would prove it.

But the officer, shrugging his shoulders, said, "This nigger is simply a swindler, sir; he has sold you what didn't belong to him. The island has long been an English possession."

In the face of this formal declaration, to which the guns of the *Tomahawk* and the bayonets of the marines added very considerable weight, Tartarin felt all discussion to be useless.

He contented himself with making his abominable father-in-law a terrible scene. "You hoary rascal, why did you tell us the island was yours? Why did you sell it to us? Do you wish to pass for a dishonest man?"

Nagonko remained speechless, goggling still more, and looking still more like a brute; his very limited and very primitive intellect having quite evaporated in the fumes of garlic and alcohol.

Tartarin, seeing he should get no sort of satisfactory answer from him, made a sign to the militiaman who had brought him—"Take him away!"

Then turning to the officer, who had remained stiff and inexpressive during the scene, "In any case, sir, my good faith is beyond question."

"The English courts of justice will settle that, sir," the other replied, from the tip-top of his superiority. "From this moment you are my prisoner. As for the inhabitants, if the island be not evacuated in the next twenty-four hours, they will all be put to the sword."

"Cracky! put to the sword!" Tartarin exclaimed. "But, in the first place, how in the world shall we evacuate—we haven't a single boat—unless we undertake to swim?"

The formidable fellow was at last brought round, and consented to carry the settlers as far towards home as Gibraltar; on condition, that is, that all arms were surrendered, even the rifles of the crack shots, the revolvers, and the thirty-two shooter.

Hereupon he went off to luncheon, leaving a squad of men to mount guard over the captive Governor.

It was also the hour of the mid-day meal at headquarters, and after having looked everywhere for his Excellency's wife, who continued to bear the title of princess, as she was nowhere to be found, not even on the top of some cocoa palm, her place was left empty.

Every one was so shaken that Brother Bataillet forgot to say grace.

The Governor and his staff had been eating some time in silence, with their noses in their plates, when suddenly Pascalon rose to his feet, and raising his glass, addressed himself to utterance.

"Gentlemen, our Go-Go-Governor is a pri-pri-prisoner of war. I needn't inquire if we shall not follow him into ca-ca-captivity!"

They sprang to their feet with uplifted glasses, shouting with enthusiasm:

"All of us—all of us!"

"Dash our eyes if we don't follow him!"

"Rather—rather!"

"Long live Tartarin! Ha! ha! ha!" howled Escourbaniès.

But in another hour they had all given him away, their poor Governor—all except Pascalon—even his little royal spouse, who had been miraculously found on the roof of the citadel.

At first she wouldn't come down; her ladies in waiting, Mademoiselle Caussemille and Mademoiselle Franquebalme, had been able to bring her to it only by the distant exhibition of an open box of sardines, just as a piece of sugar is held out to a parrot who has escaped from his cage.

"My dear child," said Tartarin, in his paternal tone, when she was again at his side, "I must tell you that I'm a prisoner of war. Which do you like best, to come with me or to stay on the island? I think the English would leave you here."

Without the least hesitation, looking at him with her smiling eyes, she replied, in her little babbling speech, as soft as the twitter of a bird, "Me tay in island; me tay always."

"Very well, you're quite free," said Tartarin, in a resigned tone.

But at bottom the poor fellow was awfully cut up.

In the evening, in the stately desert of the citadel, forsaken by his wife, by his dignitaries, and all his servants, he had only the faithful Pascalon at his side.

Through the open windows, from the distance, came the twinkle of lights in the city, the hum of the great hive, the songs of the English encamped on the shore, and the monotonous murmur of the Little Rhone, swollen by the rains.

It was all dreadfully dreary.

Tartarin closed his window again with a heavy sigh, and while he tied up his head for the night in the spotted bandana, he said to Pascalon:

"When I learned that the others were going, and that they denied me, I bore it well enough. But that little creature — I should have thought *she* would have been more attached to me."

The good Pascalon tried to console him. After all, the little savage princess would be a very queer piece of goods to carry back to Tarascon — for back to Tarascon they of course would go, if they could get there — and when Tartarin should take up his old peaceful life again, his Papuan wife might be rather in his way and bring him under notice.

"Don't you remember, my dear, kind master, that when you came back from Algeria your ca-ca-camel was rather a bother?"

"My ca-ca-camel? And pray what is there in common?"

Pascalon turned very red. What an idea to go and talk of a camel apropos of a princess of the blood royal! To make up for whatever irreverence there might have been in the comparison, he called attention to the fact that Tartarin's present situation was quite that of Napoleon after he had been taken prisoner by the English and deserted by Marie Louise.

"Quite so—quite so," said Tartarin, struck by this similitude.

And this thought that his fate had a likeness to Napoleon's had a good deal to do with consoling him—with giving him a quiet night.

The next day Port Tarascon was evacuated, to the great joy of the settlers. Their irrecoverable money, their humbugging acres, the great financial operation, the great stroke of the dirty Belgian who had victimized them—nothing of all this was worth mentioning beside their delight at getting out of their swamp.

They were all taken on board first, because in their rage against the Governor, whom they held responsible for all their ills, they might perhaps have done him a hurt.

At the moment they passed the citadel, on their way to the boats, Tartarin showed himself at his window, but he had to fall back quickly before the jeers and gibes that greeted him, and the clinched fists that were shaken at him.

On a fine day the Tarasconians would perhaps have shown him more indulgence, but the unfortunates embarked in a pouring rain, floundering in the mud, and carrying away on the soles of their shoes tons of their precious property. The bits of baggage that every one had in his hand were dreadfully exposed by the umbrellas.

When all the settlers had quitted the island the English officer came to fetch Tartarin.

At headquarters, since morning, Pascalon had been on the fidget, preparing everything, doing up into bundles the archives of the colony.

At the last hour he had a real inspiration of genius—he asked Tartarin if he shouldn't put on his mantle of Grandee of the First Class to go on board.

"Yes, let them see it; it will make an impression," replied the Governor.

And he himself put on the grand ribbon of the order.

Below, on the pavement, rang the butts of the muskets of the escort and the hard voice

of the officer—"Come, Monsieur Tartarin, we wait for your Excellency."

Before going down Tartarin took a last look around him at the house in which he had loved, in which he had suffered—known all the intensity of passion and power.

Observing at this moment that Pascalon seemed to be hiding something under his mantle of the first class, he inquired what the object might be; on which Pascalon, stuttering not a little with emotion, confessed to his kind master the existence of the *Memorial*.

"Very well; go on, my child," said Tartarin, gently, and pinched his ear as Napoleon used to pinch his grenadiers. "You shall be my little Las Casas."

The analogy of his destiny with Napoleon's had occupied his spirit all night. Yes, they were quite the same: the English, Marie, Las Casas—a real identity of circumstance and type. And both of them from the South!

BOOK THIRD.

I.

TARTARIN'S dignified mien, as he stepped on the deck of the *Tomahawk*, was not lost upon his captors. They were especially impressed by the grand ribbon of the order—pink, with the embroidered Tarasque—with which he had the odd idea of scarfing himself, as if it had been a masonic symbol, as well as with the red and black mantle of Grandee of the First Class, in which Pascalon was draped from head to foot.

The English have, in fact, beyond everything, a respect for constituted order, and even for constituted eccentricity. To be very queer, among them, is a title to esteem—it is only a question of being queer enough.

In our Algerian dependency persons animated by this respectable oddity are called *maboul*—cracked.

Half-way up the side Tartarin was received by the officer on duty, and conducted with the greatest consideration to a first-class cabin.

Pascalon was then rewarded for having followed his kind master into captivity, inasmuch as he had a room near the Governor's assigned him, instead of being thrust between the forward decks like the rest of the Tarasconians, who were huddled together as if they had been a herd of wretched emigrants. With them, in degrading promiscuity, was confined the whole of the former staff, punished in this manner for its weakness and cowardice.

Between Tartarin's cabin and that of his faithful secretary was a little saloon furnished with ottomans, embellished with panoplies and great exotic plants, and opening into a small dining-room, in which perpetual coolness was diffused from two great blocks of ice, placed in vases in the angles.

A butler and two or three footmen were attached to the person of his Excellency.

Tartarin accepted these honors without surprise, and when the officer who showed him about remarked to him in French that if he should be in want of anything he had only to ask for it, the hero replied with the "Quite so, quite so" of a sovereign accustomed to every deference, to the anticipation of his every wish.

At the moment they weighed anchor he ascended to the deck, in spite of the rain, to take a supreme leave of his island.

It rose there dimly in the broth of mist, but it was sufficiently distinct under its gray veil to yield a glimpse of King Nagonko and his ruffians engaged in pillaging the big house and dancing a frantic fandango on the shore.

All Brother Bataillet's catechumens, with the

departure of missionaries and constables, returned to the sweet spontaneity of nature.

Pascalon even thought he recognized, in the maze of the dance, the graceful silhouette of Likiriki; but of this he was not quite sure.

Leaning on the bulwarks, the hero of Tarascon looked at it all in perfect calm. The resemblance of his fate to Napoleon's had given him a kind of alabaster attitude.

This resemblance was often in his mind; he often recurred to it.

"Yes," he said to his little Las Casas, "there are strange communities between us." Like the great Emperor, he was fond of representation, of platforms and costumes. He admitted it quite frankly. "It's true, I confess, I am impressed by feathers and flourishes, by the noise and glitter of great reviews of armies—and, like him, I have been perhaps too fond of glory."

He recalled Napoleon, too, by the familiar, traditional side — a resemblance that cropped up even in little things, such as the taste for sweet dishes. He was conscious of some of its higher manifestations—the lofty and luminous eloquence—the bursts of anger, terrible and short.

"For instance, that time at the Café de la Comédie, when I had the quarrel with Costecalde. Don't you remember, Pascalon?"

And to the anecdote of the tray of Sèvres, broken one day by Napoleon, he compared the cup of coffee that he himself, in a moment of temper, had smashed at the club.

But the great point in common was the existence in each of the characteristic imagination of the South. Napoleon had it on the grand scale, and so had he; witness, on the part of his predecessor, the Egyptian campaign, all done on a camel's back, the Russian campaign, and the dream of the conquest of India. On his own side, had not his whole existence been a fabulous dream of lions and mountains, the conquest of the Jungfrau, the administration of an island five thousand leagues from France? Certainly he didn't deny that the

Emperor, from a particular point of view, was his superior; but *he* at least had not shed blood on such a scale, nor caused such terror to mankind.

Meanwhile the island disappeared in the distance, and Tartarin, still with his elbow on the bulwarks, continued to play to the gallery—to the sailors who were removing the cinders scattered on the deck, to the officers of the watch, who had drawn nearer.

At last, as Pascalon began to have enough, he asked his protector's leave to go forward and mingle with the Tarasconians, whom they perceived in a few frightened groups, in the rain, removed from them by the length of the ship. The young man pretended he wished to learn what they were saying about the Governor; but his real hope was to catch a glimpse of his dear Clorinde, and be able to drop into her ear a few words of encouragement and consolation.

An hour later, when he came back, he found Tartarin stretched on the couch in the little saloon, airing himself in his drawers, quite as if he had been at home at Tarascon, in his little house on the Long Walk, while he finished a pipe and sipped a delicious sherry-cobbler.

In a smiling mood, not the least morose, he

inquired, "Well, and what do you find those good people say about me?"

Pascalon couldn't conceal from him that it had struck him their backs were rather up.

Huddled together between the forward decks like cattle, ill fed and harshly treated, they reproached him with their principal misfortunes.

But Tartarin shrugged his shoulders. "Bah! that will all evaporate the first time the sun comes out."

He knew his people, you may well believe.

"I don't mean they really want to do anything bad," rejoined Pascalon; "but they are worked up by that scoundrel of a Costecalde."

"Costecalde! How is that?"

Tartarin was somewhat disturbed by the mention of this name. Pascalon explained to him that Costecalde, whom the *Tomahawk* had come across in mid-ocean and picked up out of a drifting boat, in which he was dying of hunger and thirst, had mentioned to the Commodore the presence of a Tarasconian colony upon English territory, and guided the ship even into port.

The eyes of the Governor flashed. "Ah, the traitor! Ah, the reprobate!"

Then Pascalon, to soothe him, related the dreadful adventures of Costecalde and his companions.

Truphénus had been drowned! The three other militiamen, going ashore somewhere to look for water, had fallen into the jaws of the anthropophagi! Barban had been found dead of starvation in the bottom of the boat! As for Rugimabaud, a shark had eaten him up.

"Come, I say, a shark! It's Costecalde who ate him up!"

"But the most extraordinary thing of all, your Ec-ec-Excellency, is that Costecalde pretends to have encountered in mid-ocean, in the midst of a storm, in the glare of the lightning —guess what?"

"What the deuce do you expect me to guess?"

"The Tarasque—the dear Old Granny!"

"Cracky, what a fraud!"

But, after all, the thing was not impossible. The *Tootoopumpum* might have been wrecked; or else the Tarasque, roped to the deck, might have been washed away by a great sea.

At this moment a steward brought his Excellency the bill of fare, and some moments later Tartarin, in the best of humor, found himself at table with Pascalon before an excellent champagne dinner—a dinner consisting of certain splendid slices of salmon and some wonderful roast beef, done to the turn, quite pink, with a delicious pudding to follow. Tartarin relished his pudding so much that he requested a substantial portion might be carried to Brother Bataillet and Franquebalme. As for Pascalon, he manufactured with the salmon and the roast beef a few delicate sandwiches, which he placed on one side. Is it necessary to say for whom, lackaday?

On the second day of the trip, as soon as the island was out of sight—it was as if its function in the archipelago had been to be an isolated reservoir of rain and fog—the weather turned fine. The ship pursued her course under a bright soft sky, through an ocean deservedly called Pacific.

Every day, after breakfast, Tartarin went above and settled himself in his place, the same place on the deck, to converse with his little Las Casas.

Here was still another point of resemblance. Had not Napoleon on the *Northumberland* his favorite corner, the cannon on which he used to lean, and which came to be called the Emperor's gun? Had the great Tarasconian this incident in mind? Was the coincidence not pure chance? It may be so; but the fact should not diminish him in our eyes. When Napoleon surrendered himself to England did *he* not think of Themistocles, think of him undisguisedly? "I come like Themistocles," and so forth, and so forth.

Who knows whom Themistocles himself was not thinking of when he came to sit by the hearth of the Persians? Humanity is so old that we are always treading in somebody's footsteps. As a matter of fact the anecdotes furnished by Tartarin to his little Las Casas, his backward glances over his career, had but a scant similarity to what is known of Napoleon, and were quite personal to himself—Tartarin of Tarascon.

His childhood in his native city figured in this retrospect: his precocious adventures; the way that, as quite a little boy, he had had the love of arms and of the chase—the love of the very smell of wild beasts. Then how, in his rashest pranks, his Latin good sense had never forsaken him, a sane inner voice saying to him: "Mind you go home early. Mind you don't take cold."

"He sat on the deck in the pleasant sun, lolled in his great rocking-chair, with a smile on his lips, and his eyes dim with memories, while at the other end of the ship peeped out the captive heads of the wretched Tarasconians. He summoned back far off things, such as a visit one day to some gypsies who had encamped near the Pont du Gard.

"The sunshine played over the red masonry, touched the great arches with fire. It was so hot, I remember, that a bottle of lemonade that I had put to cool in the river began to boil as if it were on a gas-stove. The gypsies had taken refuge in the shade of a cavern. When we were near them a ragged old crone came out to us, and after having studied the lines of my hand to tell my fortune, she said, 'Some day you'll be a king!' For a long time afterwards I attached no importance to this prophecy; I had quite forgotten it. But see how in fact it has come true!" Then, after a moment's silence, he added: "You see I drop these reminiscences helter-skelter, just as they come to me, for I think they may be useful to you for the *Memorial.*"

Pascalon drank in his hero's words, but he was not the only one to drink them. Half a dozen young midshipmen, collected round Tartarin, listened open-mouthed to his stories. Not far from them, stretched upon a bamboo couch, a young married woman, the Commodore's lady, listened as well. Of Anglo-Indian stock (Calcutta was her home), much out of health, and travelling to recover it, her warm pallor—a cheek like the petal of a magnolia—her great black eyes, gentle, pensive, profound, gave her a languid charm, the effect of which was deepened by the way a great negress in a red turban behind her waved over her head a big feather fan. The Desdemona of the ship, she slaked her thirst in the eloquence of the captive Othello.

Pascalon, very proud to see his master with such an audience, showed him off, drew him on to talk of his lion hunts, of his ascent of the Jungfrau, of the memorable siege of Pampérigouste; while Tartarin, expanding, let them have the whole thing, turn his pages like a book—some fine picture-book, illustrated by his expressive Tarasconian habit of acting whatever he said, and by the "bang! bang!" of his hunting stories.

The Anglo-Indian, in her extension-chair, as drooping as a plucked flower, and curled up in her laces to keep warm, shivered when his voice rang out, and betrayed her emotions by the pink flush in her cheek, as delicate as a faint shade of carmine in a wash of water-color.

When her husband, the Commodore, a kind of Hudson Lowe, with the head of a tiger and the cold eye of a jackal, came to say it was time to go down, she supplicated, "No, no! not yet! not yet!" edging a glance towards the great Tarasconian, who, as you may suppose, had not failed to remark her, raising his voice for her benefit, and giving another flourish to his noble attitude and accent.

Sometimes when they went down to dinner, after one of these sittings, he questioned Pascalon. "What was the Commodore's lady saying to you? It seemed to me that she was talking of me."

"Well, she was, mum-mum-master. Her ladyship was saying to me that she had already often heard you spoken of."

"That doesn't surprise me," said Tartarin, simply. "I'm very popular in England."

Still another analogy with Napoleon!

One morning, when he had gone on deck rather early, he was surprised not to find his Anglo-Indian there as usual. She had probably been kept below by the bad weather, the chill in the air that happened to have come that day. Delicate, nervously sensitive, she had shrunk from the mist and spray.

The agitation of the ocean seemed to pervade the deck itself.

There had been an excitement about a whale, an animal rare in those seas. This one had no blow-holes, and spouted no water, which led some of the sailors to declare that it was a female, and others to affirm that it was a particular species. They couldn't agree.

As the creature remained in the course of the ship, sticking close to it, a young midshipman asked leave of the Commodore to go and try to get hold of him. A surly dog, as usual, the Commodore refused, on the pretext that they had no time to lose; but he authorized the young man to try the effect of a few shots.

The presumed whale was from two hundred and fifty to three hundred yards away—now showing, now diving, rising and falling with the sea, whose perverse undulations made it very difficult to hit him.

So a few shots were taken, of which the sailors in the shrouds announced the result, or rather the absence of result, as the animal had not yet been touched. He continued to play upon the surface while every one watched, even the poor Tarasconians shivering in the forecastle, drenched, soaked, far more exposed to wind and weather than those who were quartered aft.

Standing near the young officers who were trying their skill, Tartarin pronounced on the different shots: "Too far! Too short!"

"Mum-mum-master, if *you* were to try!" bleated Pascalon.

Immediately, with a quick young impulse, one of the midshipmen turned to Tartarin.

"Would your Excellency like a shot?"

He offered his rifle, and the way Tartarin took the weapon, weighed it, and shouldered it, was something to see, as well as the way Pascalon asked, blushing, yet proud:

"How many times do you count for the whale?"

"I haven't often tried this kind," answered the hero, "but I think it's about eight."

He took aim, counted eight, fired, then returned the rifle to the officer.

"I think she has got it," said the midshipman.

"Three cheers!" cried the sailors.

"I knew it," said Tartarin, modestly.

But at this moment the air was rent with dreadful howls, frantic cries, that brought up the Commodore, who seemed to fancy his ship had suddenly been boarded by pirates. The

Tarasconians in the bows rushed about wringing their hands and brandishing their arms, all babbling together in the noise of wind and waves.

"Heaven help us, the Tarasque! He has shot the Tarasque! He has shot the dear Old Granny!"

"Cracky! what are they saying?" asked Tartarin, turning pale.

About ten yards away from the ship the Tarasque of Tarascon, the monstrous idol, reared above the green billows her slimy, scaly back, her chimera's head, with bloodshot eyes, and a ferocious laugh on her vermilion lips.

Made of some very hard wood, with a solid

skeleton, she had kept afloat with wonderful cleverness ever since the moment, as was afterwards learned, a big sea had washed her off Scrapouchinat's deck. She had been rolling hither and thither in the great tides and currents, tumbling and shining, stuck all over with sea-weed and shells, outliving the typhoon and the cyclone, never sick nor sorry—indestructible, in short—and now her first, her only wound, had been inflicted by Tartarin of Tarascon.

To come from him—and to come to her!

The great fresh gash stared at them all from the middle of the poor Old Granny's forehead.

One of the midshipmen cried: "I say, look there, Lieutenant Swift! What extraordinary beast can that be?"

"That extraordinary beast is the Tarasque, young man," said Tartarin, solemnly; "the great ancestress, the venerated grandmother, of every good Tarasconian.

The officer stared in bewilderment, as well he might, to learn that the quaint monster was related by ties of blood to the strange, swarthy, mustachioed tribe they had picked up on the shore of a desert island.

Tartarin had uncovered, humble and respectful, but the venerated grandmother was already far, tumbling through the wide swell of the

Pacific. There she must wander still, an unsubmergable waif, mentioned here and there, from time to time, in travellers' tales, now as a gigantic polypus, now as a huge sea-serpent, and ever the terror of crews and the stupefaction of whalers.

As long as she was within sight Tartarin followed her, in silence, with his eyes; and only when she became at last a little black spot on the white surge of the horizon he murmured, feebly, to Pascalon, "Remember, *I* have told you, my child, that's a shot that will bring me bad luck!"

And all the rest of the day the hero was uneasy, full of remorse and of a kind of sacred dread.

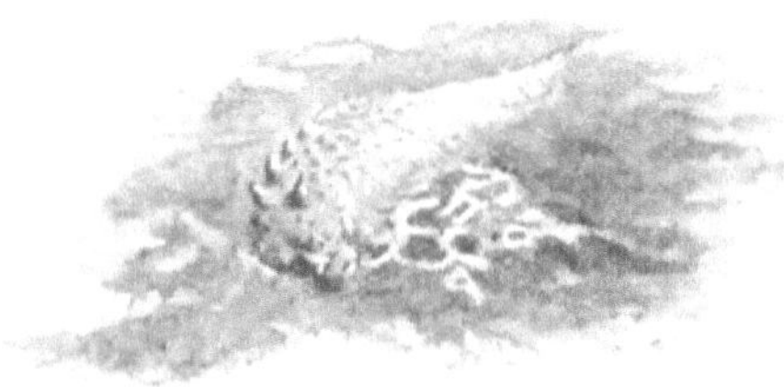

II.

They had been sailing for a week, and were approaching the fragrant shores of India under the same clear and creamy sky, on the same soft, oily sea, that Tartarin had enjoyed on his first voyage, when, on a fine afternoon of heat and light, he was dozing in his cabin, in linen pantaloons, his dear old head done up in his spotted bandanna, knotted like the peaceful ears of a ruminant.

Suddenly Pascalon tumbled into the room.

"Eh? What is it? What's the matter?" the great man broke out, pulling off his bandanna, which he was not fond of exhibiting.

"I th-th-think she's done for!" answered Pascalon, out of breath, rounding his eyes and stammering more than ever.

"Who's done for?—the Tarasque? Devil take her, I know it too well!"

"No, no," said Pascalon, below his breath; "I speak of the Commodore's lady."

"Mercy on us! poor little thing—she too? What makes you think so?"

For all answer Pascalon held out to him an engraved card, nothing less than an invitation to dinner that very evening from Commodore Lord William and Lady William Plantagenet—an invitation including his Excellency's secretary.

"Oh, the old story—woman! woman!" Tartarin cried; for evidently this invitation must have proceeded from her ladyship. The idea could not have been the husband's; he didn't deal in such delicate attentions. "However, ought I to accept? Doesn't my position of prisoner of war—"

Pascalon, who had chapter and verse, reminded him that on the *Northumberland* Napoleon ate at the Admiral's table.

"Yes, that settles it," Tartarin instantly rejoined.

"Only the Emperor used to retire with the ladies when the wine came on," Pascalon added.

"Perfectly! that settles it still better. Reply, in the third person, that we shall have the pleasure of going."

"And we dress, master, don't we?"

"Certainly we dress!"

Pascalon would have liked to drape himself

in his mantle of Grandee of the First Class, but Tartarin did not favor this measure, not intending himself to assume the ribbon of the Order.

"The invitation is not to the Governor; it is to Tartarin," he said to his secretary. "Don't you see the shade?"

There was nothing that the deuce of a fellow didn't himself see.

The dinner was truly princely; served in a great glittering saloon that was furnished in the rarest woods, and ceiled and wainscoted in that deft and delicate English panelling in which the fitting of the firm thin plates is like goldsmith's work.

Tartarin was seated in the place of honor, on Lady William's right. There were few guests —only Lieutenant Swift and the ship's doctor, both of whom understood French. A footman in nankeen livery, stiff and solemn, stood behind every chair. Nothing could have been richer than the decanters and flagons and wine-coolers, the massive plate with the Plantagenet arms. In the middle of the table was a magnificent piece of silver overflowing with the choicest flowers. You might have thought you were dining with a viceroy.

Pascalon, naturally bashful in all this splendor, stuttered the more that he always happened to have his mouth full when he tried to speak. He admired the easy grace of Tartarin under the observation of their tigerish host, who rolled suspicious eyes, green eyes injected with blood, and not rendered more human by albino brows and lashes. This had not the least effect on Tartarin: it was easy to see he was used to creatures of the jungle. He talked to Lady William with high courtesy, he chatted and gesticulated, while his hostess scarcely made an effort to conceal her sympathy for the hero, looking at him with such orbs of her own, extraordinary orbs, that seemed at once to laugh and to languish.

"The unfortunates! The husband will see it all!" Pascalon said to himself every moment.

Her ladyship desired to know all about the wonderful Tarasque.

So Tartarin told her the old tale of St. Martha and her blue ribbon; told her of his people, the history of the Tarasconian race, its traditions, and its exodus. Then he gave her a sketch of his administration, his projects, his reforms, the new code of law that he had drawn up. It was an odd thing, but it happened to be the first time he had ever spoken of his code of law.

He was profound; he was bantering; and, grazing as he went the things of the heart, he sang a few of the airs of his country—about John of Tarascon, for instance, taken by Corsairs, and his romantic amours with the Sultan's daughter.

Leaning over Lady William, with what eyes he devoured her as he sang the verse:

"They say that when he became general of the army,
With laurels on his brow, the laurels of the victor,
The daughter of the king, the daughter sweet and shining,
Said to him, for she was smitten," etc.

He amused and delighted them all; they all relaxed and thawed under the influence of his warm, sonorous voice.

Her languid ladyship, usually so pale, turned quite rosy.

She asked him about the national reel, the famous *farandole*, that he was always talking about.

"Dear me, it's simple enough. I'll see if I can't show you."

And wishing to monopolize the effect, he said to his secretary, "No, Pascalon; don't get up!"

He himself got up, striking out as he hummed the air—ra-pa-ta, pa-ta-pla! Unhappily at this moment the ship gave a lurch, so that he presently found himself in a sitting posture on the floor; but he picked himself up good-humoredly, and was the first to laugh at his misadventure.

The Englishry were tickled to death. The banquet at this moment was drawing to a close—poor Tartarin had scarcely tasted it—and as the decanters had been ranged on the board, her ladyship rose and rustled out.

At this the Tarasconian instantly tossed away his napkin and followed her, without explanation or excuse—conforming thus, in every particular, to Napoleonic tradition. This was what Napoleon did; so why shouldn't *he* do it?

The English looked at each other in stupefaction, and exchanged in their language a few remarks that Pascalon only vaguely understood, such as "original," "awfully queer," "off his head."

The good secretary did his best to apologize for his master; put forward the plea that his Excellency, who scarcely drank any wine, was never in the habit of sitting long.

Then, as Tartarin was out of the way, it became his turn to let himself go. Pascalon took the floor and kept it. He told a series of stories of his own, and on the question of claret was quite a match for his entertainers. You wouldn't have recognized these starched gentry under the contagious, humanizing, Southern influence of the two Tarasconians.

Shrewdly suspecting that his kind master had gone to rejoin her ladyship on deck, Pascalon, as soon as they rose from table, offered to take a hand with the Commodore, whom he knew to be a devotee of chess.

Their companions conversed roundabout, and at a given moment Mr. Swift said something to the doctor that made him laugh aloud.

The Commodore raised his head: "What is Swift saying that's clever?"

Swift repeated what he had said, and the pair laughed again.

Pascalon easily made out that they were talking of Tartarin, but he could only catch a few words; the sense was lost to him.

Meanwhile, what was Tartarin up to?

He was on the deck, close to his hostess, and the minutes elapsed for him with a charm and a sweetness of their own. They drew an irresistible poetry from the warm, scented breath of the trade-winds, and from the rich glow on sky and sea, and all over the deck of the ship, of a great sunset that made all the ropes and spars seem to trickle with gooseberry juice. Leaning against Lady William's chair, our gallant friend, who habitually wore his heart slung over his shoulder, took advantage of the hour for reverie, the hour for love; he bent towards his companion and murmured low. Knowing how women like to comfort and console, he related, in a voice muffled with emotion, the romance of his relations with the little dusky princess. Pulling off the plaster, as it were, from the sore of his grief, he drew a picture of their heart-rending separation.

I won't declare to you that the picture was very exact, that he didn't compose and arrange it a little; but, at any rate, he painted the scene as he would have liked it to be. The "poor child" had been dragged one way by family duties and the other by conjugal love; so that, with his crushed heart, he could only bid her remain with her old father, who had no one else left. As he told these things he shed real tears, and it seemed to him there were tears, too, in the fine Anglo-Indian eyes that rested on him while the sun slowly sank into the sea, leaving on the horizon a kind of violet bloom.

But shadows approach, and the freezing voice of the Commodore suddenly breaks the spell:

"It's getting late; it's too cool for you, my dear. You must go down."

She got up, and bowed slightly. "Good-night, Monsieur Tartarin."

He was infinitely

moved by the softness with which these words were uttered.

He remained a few minutes longer on the deck, walking to and fro, alone with his thoughts; but night was rapidly coming on. The Commodore was right; the air was beginning to freshen; so he thought it best to go to bed.

In passing the little saloon, of which the door was ajar, he noticed Pascalon seated at a table with his head in his hands, and the appearance of turning with great intensity the leaves of a lexicon.

"What are you doing there, my Pascalon?"

The faithful secretary, following him into his cabin, apprised him of the scandal caused by his abrupt withdrawal from the table. He spoke of the phrase dropped by Lieutenant Swift and overheard by the Commodore, who had made him repeat it, to the general amusement.

"Although I understand English tolerably well," said Pascalon, "I didn't quite catch the meaning of it. I only understood that they were talking of something like a garden globe—one of those big balls, silvered over, you know, that stand on a lawn, and reflect surrounding objects. But, as I remembered the words, I've just been trying to reconstruct the sentence."

While these explanations went on Tartarin had lain down and stretched himself out in his bed, quite at his ease, with his head done up in his bandanna; and he asked, while he lighted the pipe that he smoked every night before he went to sleep, "And how, then, does your translation come out?"

"This way, my dear master—this is it: On the whole, the Tarasconian is the Frenchman magnified and exaggerated—seen, as it were, in a garden globe."

"And you tell me that was what they found to laugh at?"

"All of them—the Lieutenant, the doctor, the Commodore himself. They could scarcely stop laughing."

Tartarin shrugged his shoulders with a grimace of pity. "It tells the story of how rarely the English have occasion to laugh, if that sort of rubbish amuses them. Come, good-night, my child; go to bed yourself."

And soon they were both lapped in dreams—dreams in which one communed with his Clorinde, and the other with the Commodore's lady—for Likiriki was already of the past.

The days followed the days and made up

weeks, and the voyage stretched out, adorable, divine—an episode to count in Tartarin's life.

Ah! they were unforgettable hours—such hours as one wishes to keep forever, to fix there with a golden pin, as you fix a butterfly in a glass case; made up of long talks on the deck, and of unexpressed affection for a charming listening woman, of whom one asked nothing more than the sympathy she had already shown.

Add to this the natural attraction that he exercised on all round him, officers and sailors alike having nothing for him but kind smiles. It was he who might have said, as Victor Jacquemont* said in his correspondence: "How odd is my fortune with the English! These men who seem so inexpressive among themselves, always so cold and dumb, my communicativeness never fails to make them unbend. They become affectionate in spite of themselves, and for the first time in their lives I make capital kind people—I make Frenchmen—of any Englishmen with whom I spend twenty-four hours"

If an ordinary Frenchman could effect this magical transformation, only think what a Tarasconian might have done, being a Frenchman mul-

* The celebrated French traveller.

tiplied by ten!—what Tartarin, above all, could do, being a complete compendium of Tarascon!

He was adored by every one on the ship—that is, by every one in the cabin. There was no more talk of his being a prisoner of war—of his taking his chance with an English jury.

It was quite settled that he was to be set free as soon as they should reach Gibraltar.

As for the fierce Commodore, delighted to have found an adversary as redoubtable as Pascalon, he passed half his days before the chess-board, leaving Tartarin in full liberty to make a certain degree of love to Lady William.

The poor secretary was the only one who was not perfectly happy. He found these interminable games of chess a dreadful bondage, so that he was even sorry to have betrayed his skill. He was much disconcerted in the evening, in particular, when he found himself, through having to give the Commodore his eternal *revanche*, prevented from going forward to take a look at his dear Clorinde, for whom he never failed to put aside some delicate morsel, some tidbit purloined from the Governor's dessert.

For our poor Tarasconians, on their side, continued to be treated as prisoners, and huddled far forward in their gallery; so that it was the only sadness Tartarin knew, the wrinkle in his bed of roses, when he was perorating on the poop, or making a certain degree of love in the pensive glow of the sunset, the fact that over against him there, below the level of the lifted stern, he had a glimpse of his compatriots jammed together like vile cattle, under the guard of a sentry, and that they averted their eyes from him in horror, especially after the baleful day when he pointed a rifle at the Tarasque.

They could never forgive him this crime, nor could he himself ever forget the fatal shot that was to bring him bad luck.

They had passed the Strait of Malacca, the Red Sea, and had rounded the Sicilian cape; they were getting on to Gibraltar.

One morning, as land had been sighted, Tartarin and Pascalon were putting up their luggage, with the help of one of the footmen, when suddenly they became conscious of the little lurch given by a ship when it stops. The *Tomahawk* was stopping, in fact, and at the same moment was heard a sound of oars.

"See what it is, Pascalon," said Tartarin. "Isn't it probably the pilot?"

A row-boat had hailed them, indeed, but it was not the pilot, as the boat carried the French flag, and was manned by French sailors, among whom were visible two men dressed in black and wearing high hats.

The soul of Tartarin thrilled. "Ah, the French flag! Let me see it—let me see it, my child."

He made for the port-hole, but at this moment the door opened, admitting a flood of light, and two constables in plain clothes, with brutal voices, armed with warrants, with a writ of extradition, with all the tackle, in short, laid their base hands on the unhappy State of Things and on his secretary. The State of Things turned pale and retreated. "Take

care what you do! I'm Tartarin of Tarascon!"

"That's just why!"

There was not a further word of explanation; not a word of reply to his multiplied questions. It was impossible to learn what either of them had done, why they were arrested, and where they were to be conducted. It was impossible to learn anything, to become conscious of anything but the shame of passing laden with chains—for they had been handcuffed—before the midshipmen and the sailors, and through the laughter and jeers of hooting compatriots, who leaned over the sides of the ship, and applauded, and cried, "Bravo! well done! zou, zou!" as the captives were let down to the boat.

At this moment Tartarin would have liked to sink to the bottom of the sea.

To change from a prisoner of war like Napoleon to the condition of a vulgar swindler! And the Commodore's lady looked on!

Decidedly he was right—the Tarasque was avenged, was even cruelly avenged.

III.

July 5th. Prison of Tarascon-on-the Rhone. —I'm just back from the preliminary inquiry. I know, at last, of what we are accused, the Governor and I, and why, brutally seized on the *Tomahawk*, in the midst of bliss, like a pair of eels plucked out of the clear depths, we were transferred to a French ship, and brought in handcuffs to Marseilles, whence, under the pressing attentions paid to accomplished criminals, we were forwarded to Tarascon, and placed in solitary confinement in the city jail.

We are accused of gross fraud, of manslaughter through criminal neglect, and of violating the laws on emigration. Ah, most certainly I must have violated them, the laws on emigration, for it's the very first time I've ever heard of them, even by name, confound them!

After two days of solitary confinement, and being forbidden to speak to any one whatever —that's the sort of thing that's terrible for one

of *us*—we were dragged to the police-court and planted there before a magistrate.

This magistrate, Monsieur Bonicar by name, began his career at Tarascon some ten years ago, so that he knows me perfectly, having been more than a hundred times at the shop, where I used to prepare him a dressing for a chronic eczema that he had on his face, and that he still has.

This didn't prevent him, however, from asking me my surname and my Christian name, my age and my profession, as if he had never seen me in his life. I had to tell him everything I knew about the Port Tarascon business, and to talk two hours without drawing breath. I went so fast his clerk couldn't follow me. Then, without good-morning or good-evening, "Accused, you may step down."

In the lobby of the court I encountered my poor Governor, whom I had not seen since the day we were put under lock and key. He struck me as terribly changed.

As I passed he managed to say to me, in that voice of his that thrills: "Courage, my child! The truth is like oil; it always rises to the surface."

He couldn't add another word: the constables hustled him away.

Constables for him! Tartarin in irons at Tarascon! And this anger, this hatred of a whole people—*his* people!

I shall always have in my ears their howls of fury, the hot breath of the Rabblebabble when the police van brought us back here, each of us padlocked in his compartment.

The lowered hood of my kennel prevented me from seeing, but I could hear all round me the uproar of a great crowd. There was a moment when the van stopped in the middle of the market-place. I knew this by the smell that came in through the cracks, by the little gleams of sweet light; it was the very breath of the city, an odor of love-apples, egg-plant, melons of Cavaillon, pepper-plant, and great sweet onions. Oh, how it made my mouth water to smell all the good things that I haven't touched for such an age!

There was such a dense crowd that our horses couldn't get on—a Tarascon crammed full enough to make you believe that nobody had ever been killed, or drowned, or devoured by the anthropophagi. Didn't I even seem to recognize the voice of our Assessor of Taxes, the late Cambalalette? It was an illusion, certainly, inasmuch as Bézuquet himself is able to testify to the taste of the poor man's flesh; but all the same it will give you an idea. One thing I certainly heard, a most familiar jabber: "Duck him! drown him! Zou, zou! To the Rhone! to the Rhone! Let's make a noise! To the river with Tartarin!" Escourbaniès was not to be mistaken; he was yelling louder than any one.

To the river with Tartarin! What a lesson in history! What a page for the *Memorial!*

I forgot to say that our examining magistrate gave me back my diary, which had been seized on the *Tomahawk*. He had found it interesting; he even urged me to continue it; and in regard to a few of our local idioms which have slipt in here and there, he said to me, as he smiled in his red whiskers, "You shouldn't call it the *Petit Mémorial:* you should call it the *Petit Méridional!*"

I pretended to laugh at his wretched joke.

July 5th–15th.—The city prison at Tarascon is an old historic castle, the former castle of King René, which you may see any day from a distance on the bank of the Rhone, flanked with its four towers.

We have not had much luck with old historic castles. That time in Switzerland when my illustrious friend was taken for a Nihilist leader, and we were all taken with him, didn't they throw us, at Chillon, into the dungeon of Bonivard?

Here, it is true, it is a little less miserable the sunshine pours in, tempered with the breeze of the Rhone; it's not perpetually raining, like Switzerland and Port Tarascon.

My place of confinement is of the narrowest; the four bare stone walls, with a few inscriptions gouged out, an iron bedstead, a table, and a chair. I get my sun through a barred window—anything but "big"—that hangs high over the Rhone.

It's just from here that during the great Revolution the Jacobins were chucked into the river—those for whom they made our famous popular song.

Dear me, how the populace never changes! They favor us in the evening with that terrible catch. I hear their voices come up from below. I don't know what they've done with my poor Governor, but the horrid chorus must reach him as well as me, and he must make some singular reflections.

My dearest master! how, with his expansive nature, he must miss me! And I miss him too, though I confess I feel a certain relief at being alone and able to think things over.

In the long-run it's rather fatiguing to be intimate with a great man. He talks so much about himself! That was why, on the *Tomahawk*, I never had a minute of my own, never an instant to take a look at my Clorinde. So, many a time I said to myself, "She's over there!" but I could never get away. After dinner I always had the Commodore's confounded chess, and the rest of the day Tartarin never let go of me, especially after I confessed to him that I was busy with the *Memorial*. "Write down this. Don't forget to make a note of that." He poured out anecdotes about himself and his relations, and they were not always particularly interesting.

To think of poor Las Casas! Of his having driven such a trade for so many years! The

Emperor used to wake him up at six in the morning to carry him off to walk, to drive, and as soon as they had started, used to begin: "Have you got the place, Las Casas? When I signed the treaty of Campo-Formio—" The poor confidant had his own affairs—his sick child, his wife in France—but what was this for the other, who thought of nothing but describing and explaining himself to Europe, to the universe, to posterity, every day and all day, every night and all night, for years and years together? The truth is, the real victim of the English was not Napoleon, but Las Casas.

At present, however, I'm spared this tribulation. Heaven bear me witness that I've not worked for my independence. It is only that they keep us apart, and I take advantage of it to think of myself, of my infinite misery, and of my beloved Clorinde.

Does she believe me guilty? She—never! But her family does—all the Espazettes and the Escudelles de Lambesc. For all that set a man without a title is always guilty. In any case I've given up all hope of ever being accepted as a candidate for the dear girl's hand, fallen as I am from earthly grandeurs. I shall have to go and take up my work again among

Bézuquet's bottles and jars, in the pharmacy on the bit of a square. Such is glory!

July 17th.—A thing that troubles me much is that no one comes to see me. They include me in the hatred that they cherish for my master. As the proverb says,

> "When the wind is straight, the tree bends,
> When a man's poor, he lacks friends."

My cell affords me no other recreation than an occasional perch on my table. In this way I can reach my window, from which, through the iron grating, I catch a wonderful view.

Between its little pale green islands, brushed up with the breeze, the Rhone is shot with scattered sunshine, while the sky is all streaked with the dark flight of the martens, rushing about with little cries, almost grazing me, or dropping from ever so far up. Far below me is the great suspension-bridge, so long that it swings like a hammock; you expect to see it whisked away like somebody's hat as soon as the mistral blows, as indeed you might have seen it once upon a time.

On the banks of the river rise the ruins of old castles—Beaucaire, with the town at its feet, and Courtezon too, and Vacqueiras. Behind their thick walls, crumbling with age, were held of old those courts of love in which the troubadours, the national bards of those days, enjoyed the favor of the princesses and queens they sang. How everything changes! The old manors are now but heaps of stone smothered in briers, and the national bards of to-day may sing about the fine ladies and the damsels as they will, the damsels and the fine ladies don't trouble their heads about them.

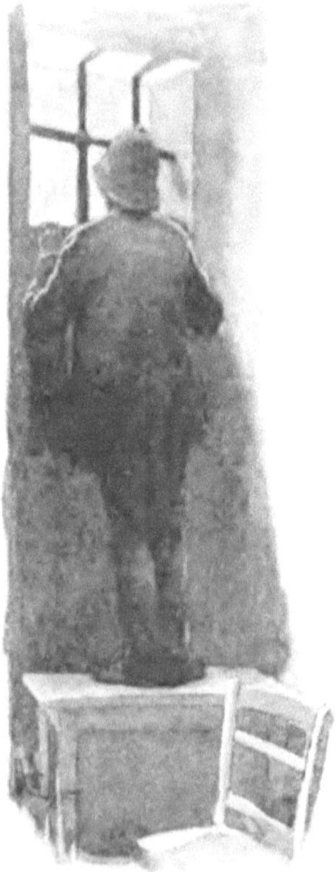

A glimpse that makes me rather less sad is that of the Beaucaire Canal, with all its boats massed together, and on its borders the red legs of the little soldiers whom from my casement I see strolling about.

The good people of Beaucaire must be delighted with all our misadventures, and especially with the collapse of our great man. It must be a joy to them to know he's in prison, and treated like a thief fit for hanging or drowning, for our proud opposite neighbors have long been exasperated by his renown—ever since they have ceased to be heard of themselves, and their famous fair has ceased to be talked about.

When I was a boy I remember what a rumpus they still used to make with that great invention. People flocked from all over (except from Tarascon—the bridge is so dangerous); it was a tremendous concourse, half a million of souls at the least, crammed in between the booths. But from year to year the thing has gone off; it's nothing to speak of now. Beaucaire still holds her great fair, only no one comes to it. You see nothing but placards up in the place: To Let; To Let; Furnished Apartments; so that if some traveller does turn up, a stray bagman or so, the people all rush out and overwhelm him, rend him limb from limb. The Town Council comes to meet him with a band of music. In a word, Beaucaire has lost every sort of credit, while Tarascon has grown more and more celebrated; and thanks to whom, pray, if not to Tartarin?

Perched on my table, just now, I was looking out and thinking of these things. The sun had gone down, it was twilight, when suddenly, on the other side of the Rhone, a great light was kindled on the tower of their castle. It burned a long time, and a long time I watched it; for it struck me it was rather mysterious, this arbitrary blaze, casting a ruddy reflection on the Rhone in the deep silence of the night, stirred only by the heavy flight of the buzzard. What could it be meant for?—was it a signal?

Is there some one, some admirer of our great Tartarin, who wants to help him to escape? It's so extraordinary, such a blaze lighted on the very top of a ruined tower, just opposite to his prison!

July 18th.—To-day, as we came back from the court, while the police van was passing before St. Martha's, I heard the still imperious voice of Madame des Espazettes call out, with the familiar nasality of these parts, "Cloreinde! Clorinde!" and a soft, angelic voice, the voice of my beloved, reply, "Mamma-a-a!" She's so lamb-like that she seemed to ba-a it.

I dare say she was on her way to church to pray for me, for the issue of the trial.

Returned to prison greatly touched. Wrote a few verses in our graceful dialect on the happy presage of this encounter.

In the evening, at the same hour, the same fire blazes on the tower of Beaucaire. It shines over there in the darkness like the bonfire always kindled on St. John's Eve. Evidently it's a signal.

Tartarin, with whom I have been able to exchange two words in the lobby, has also seen the mysterious flame through the bars of his dungeon, and when I told him what I thought of it, suggested that it may be the work of friends who wish, like those of Napoleon at St. Helena, to get him away, he seemed greatly struck by the parallel.

"Ah, really, when Napoleon was at St. Helena they tried to rescue him!"

But after a moment's reflection he declared that he would never consent to this.

"It's not the descent from the tower—the descent of three hundred feet by a rope-ladder—that would frighten me. Don't think that, my child! What I should dread much more is looking as if I were afraid to meet the charge. Tartarin of Tarascon will never flee!"

Ah, if all those who keep howling as he passes, "To the river, zou! to the Rhone!" could have heard with what sincerity of accent he spoke! And they accuse him of gross fraud; they pretend to believe him an accomplice of the infamous Duc de Mons! Oh, come, you don't mean it!

It's none the less true that he no longer

stands up for his duke; he now estimates the Belgian scoundrel at his true value. This will clearly appear from his defence, for Tartarin is to plead his own cause. For myself, I stutter too much to speak in public; so my case has been undertaken by Cicero Franquebalme, the incomparably and inveterately close texture of whose reasoning is a secret to nobody.

July 20th. Evening.—The hours that I pass before the magistrate are dreadfully painful. The difficulty is not to defend myself, but to do it without too utterly giving away my poor master. He has been so imprudent, has had such blind confidence in his abominable duke. And then, with the intermittent eczema of the worthy on the bench, one never knows whether to fear or to hope; for his affection rides him like a mania—he is furious when it "shows," though he lets you off easier when it doesn't.

An individual on whom it "shows," on whom it will always "show," is our unfortunate Bézuquet, who, over there on our far isle, used to get on well enough with his pictorial punctures; but here, under the sky of Provence, is so sorry for himself that he never goes out; buries himself in the depths of his laboratory, where he mixes herbs and makes messes, serving his customers in a velvet mask, like a conspirator in a comic opera.

It is noticeable that men are much more sensitive than women to these cutaneous affections —eruptions and pimples and blotches. I dare say this is at the bottom of Bézuquet's rancor against Tartarin—the cause of all his woes.

July 24th.—Summoned before M. Bonicar again. I think it must be the last time. He showed me a bottle that had been found by a fisherman on one of the islands of the Rhone, and made me read a letter that the bottle contained:

"TARTARIN, Tarascon, City Jail. Courage. A friend is looking out for you at the other end of the bridge. He will cross it when the moment has come.

"A FELLOW-VICTIM OF THE DUC DE MONS."

The magistrate asked me if I remembered to have seen this handwriting before. I replied that I didn't know it; but, as one must always tell the truth, I added that an attempt had once been made to correspond with Tartarin on some such system. I spoke of the similar bottle that before our great exodus reached him with a letter to which he had attached no importance, judging it only a rather vulgar joke.

The magistrate said, "Very good," and thereupon dismissed me.

July 26th. The inquiry is over, and the case is expected to come on very soon. The town is in high fermentation. The case will be opened about August 1st. There will be little sleep for me till then. It's long, moreover, since I have really slept in this roasting little oven of a cell. I'm obliged to leave the window open, so that the mosquitoes come in in clouds. I also have the pleasure of hearing the rats crunching in the corners.

During these last days I have had several interviews with my counsel. He speaks of Tartarin with infinite bitterness. I feel that he doesn't forgive him for not having intrusted him with his case. Poor Tartarin! he has no one on his side.

It seems that the whole composition of the court has been altered. Franquebalme has given me the names of the judges: Mr. Justice Mouillard, with Van Iceberg and Roger du Nord for assistants. There's no local influence to work. I'm told these gentlemen don't come from here. For some reason unknown to me, the charges of manslaughter through criminal neglect and violation of the laws on Emigration have been withdrawn from the indictment. A warrant is out against our precious duke, but I shall be surprised to see him turn up; so that Tartarin will have beside him in the dock only Pascal Testanière, known as Pascalon.

July 31st.—A night of fever and anguish. It comes on to-morrow. Lay very late in bed. Had only strength to jot down this Tarasconian proverb that I used to hear repeated by Bravida—he knew them all:

"To stay in bed and not to sleep,
To wait and yet see nothing peep,
To love and yet have no delight—
Are things to kill a man outright."

IV.

MERCY on us, no, they didn't come from there, poor Tartarin's judges, as you might have seen on the fine August afternoon when the case was opened in the great crowded court-room.

I must tell you that the month of August, at Tarascon, is the climax of the oppressive heat; it's as hot as Africa, and the precautions against the vertical blaze of the sky are very much the same. The recall of the troops is sounded at eleven in the morning; from that hour till four o'clock they never stir out; even the cavalry are confined to barracks. You may therefore imagine the temperature of a court-room stuffed with an inquisitive public, packed so close that no one could budge, with all the ladies, in feathers and furbelows, piled in the gallery at the end.

Two o'clock rang out from the old clock-face, with the images that go in and out, on the town-hall; and through the high windows, flung wide open and draped in long yellow curtains that acted as blinds, broke the deafening shrill of the cicadas in the tropical-looking trees of the Long Walk—big trees with white, dusty leaves. This sound was accompanied by the uproar of the crowd, who couldn't get in, and by the cry of the water-venders, familiar in the bull-baiting days in the old Roman arena that does duty at Tarascon as a modern circus: "Water, fresh water—who'll have a glass?" This was a much more interesting spectacle than even the bull-baiting, and the public trial of the great Tartarin drew an audience from the whole country, from Nîmes, from Arles, from Avignon, even from Marseilles.

But you had to be from Tarascon to resist the heat, the sort of heat in which a man under sentence of death (if he be not a native) goes to sleep while it's pronounced. The most prostrate of all were the three judges, especially Mr. Justice Mouillard, from Lyons, with an air of austerity, and a long, hoary, philosophic head which made him look, if not like a French Swiss, at least like a Swiss Frenchman, and the mere sight of which filled you with a desire to weep. The very names of his two coadjutors, Van Iceberg and Roger du Nord, sufficiently attest how little they also were to the manor born.

At the very beginning of the business these three sages sank, in spite of themselves, into a vague torpor, fixing their eyes on the great squares of light cut out behind the yellow curtains, and ending by undisguised slumber during the interminable roll-call of the witnesses, at least two hundred and fifty in number, and all for the prosecution.

The constables, who didn't come from there either, and who had been cruelly left to sweat under their heavy toggery, also slept the sleep of the just; the very flies, the terrible full-blown flies of midsummer, slept in their swarms on the ceiling.

These were certainly very bad conditions for dispensing true justice. Happily the judges had studied the case in advance; without that they wouldn't have understood a word of it, as in their dozing vagueness they heard nothing but the racket of the cicadas and a far-off hum of voices.

After all the witnesses had filed past the Public Prosecutor, Monsieur Bompard du Mazet, began to read the indictment.

This time, I grant you, you have nothing to do with the North. Imagine a little hairy dwarf, with a paunch, all made up of a black crop and a black beard, and of starts and jumps and popping eyes, the instruments of a perpetual pantomime, in which he indulged as freely as if his great hot snoring voice didn't split your ears like a brass-band. When he cried he shed real tears, as big as peas; when he laughed his huge reverberating guffaw caught up the farthest man in the crowd stationed under the open doors and windows.

He passed for the glory of the Tarascon bar; but what rendered his requisitory still more interesting, what gave it a peculiar attraction, was the relationship of the orator to the hapless Bompard, one of the first victims of the sad episode of Port Tarascon.

Never did an accuser seem to thirst more for the blood of his victims. Lord, how he treated our poor Tartarin, seated there with his secretary between two constables; how dear he made him pay for his past triumphs!

Pascalon, overwhelmed with shame and despair, hid his head in his hands; but Tartarin, superior to that sort of thing, calm and decorous, listened to everything, endured everything, conscious of his decline, but also of the purity of his motives and the stainlessness of his honor. Meanwhile M. Bompard du Mazet, more and more insulting, held him up as a vulgar impostor who had taken advantage of a reputation that would bear no scrutiny—of lions that he perhaps never killed, of mountains that he perhaps never climbed, to associate himself with an adventurer, an obscure if pretended duke, who had not even an address to give the authorities. He represented Tartarin as even more guilty than the duke himself, inasmuch as the mysterious stranger could not be accused of having plucked his own countrymen. The peculiar infamy of Tartarin was to have speculated on the Tarasconians, to have stripped them to their skins, scattering ruin and misery round. "However," the orator demanded, "what could you have expected of the man who would fire upon the blessed Tarasque, upon our general grandmother?"

At this peroration there was a burst, from the benches, of patriotic sobs, which were reechoed in howls from the streets, where the

Prosecutor's voice had been heard; and he himself, moved to tears by his own eloquence, began to choke and sputter so loud that the judges woke up with a start. Bompard du Mazet had spoken for two hours.

At this moment, though the heat was still very great, a tiny fresh breeze from the Rhone began to flutter in at the windows.

Mr. Justice Mouillard now managed to stay awake; to keep him so, indeed (for he had only lately been called to Tarascon), his growing bewilderment would soon have sufficed, so abundantly was it fed by the inventive genius of the Tarasconians, their unconscious and imperturbable mendacity.

The principal accused was the first to set this wonderful spirit in motion.

During a portion of his examination, which we are obliged to abbreviate, Tartarin suddenly raised to heaven his extended hand:

"I swear before heaven and all the company that I never wrote a word of that letter!"

The letter was the letter he had sent from Marseilles to Pascalon, then editor of the *Gazette*, to wind him up, to make him lay it on a little thicker.

Well, now it appeared that Tartarin had never written it; he absolutely denied and he

energetically protested. Perhaps the so-called duke, not present—

Here Monsieur Mouillard interrupted him:

"Please hand this letter to the accused."

Tartarin took it, looked at it, then replied, quite simply:

"Oh yes, I see it is my hand. I did write it, but I couldn't just remember!"

A moment later came a similar performance on the part of Pascalon, in regard to an article in the *Gazette* describing the great reception at the town-hall of Port Tarascon—the reception of the passengers of the *Farandole* and the *Lucifer* by King Nagonko, the natives, and the first settlers, accompanied with many details about this civic edifice, of which, as we know, not a brick had ever been laid.

Pascalon listened to the reading of this effusion, which provoked the crowd to inextinguishable laughter and still more inextinguishable ire; he himself was indignant, not a word of it was his, never in his life had he put his signature to such a pack of lies.

They placed before his eyes the printed article, signed with his name and illustrated with little pictures based on hints he had given, together with his manuscript, which had been picked up at the printer's.

"It's crushing," the unhappy youth then admitted, stuttering and weeping; "it had completely escaped my mind!"

Tartarin took up the defence of his secretary:

"The truth is, my lord, that, believing blindly

all the stories told by the person De Mons, not present—"

"He has a broad back, the person De Mons, not present," the Prosecutor interpolated.

"I gave to this unhappy child," Tartarin continued, "the idea of an article to be made of them, saying to him, 'Now embroider on that.' And he embroidered."

"It is true that I never did anything but embroi-broi-broider!" Pascalon timidly panted.

Oh, of the art of embroidery, Monsieur Mouillard was not to want for specimens, now that he had begun the examination of the witnesses, all from Tarascon and all inventive, denying to-day exactly the thing they had categorically affirmed yesterday.

"But this was what you said in the preliminary inquiry."

"I? *I* said that? I never opened my mouth!"

"But you signed it."

"*I? I* signed it?"

"Here is your signature."

"Lord love us—it's true! Very well, no one can be more surprised than I!"

It was just the same for all of them—no one remembered anything about anything. The judges turned wan, sat confounded and bewildered at this appearance of flagrant bad faith, unable, in their character of men of the North, to make the allowances indispensable in the case of the South—to make so many fantastic declarations and negations square in the least with the facts.

One of the most extraordinary depositions was that of Costecalde, when he related how he had been driven from the island, forced to abandon his wife and children, by the exactions of Tartarin, romantically represented as a ferocious tyrant. Nothing could be more exciting, more thrilling, than his adventure in the long-boat, the frightful successive deaths of his unhappy companions. He sobbed as he depicted the last moments of Rugimabaud, swimming near the boat to freshen himself up a little, then abruptly gobbled up by a shark, cut quite in two.

"Ah, my poor friend's smile—I see it still! He held out his arms to me, and I was dashing towards him, when suddenly his face is contorted, he disappears; nothing is left, nothing but a circle of blood that spreads over the surface of the water." And with his clinched hand Costecalde sketched a great circle in the air.

Hearing the name of Rugimabaud, the two justices Van Iceberg and Roger du Nord, roused but a moment before from their slumberous gloom, leaned towards their colleague, so that amid the unanimous outburst of sobs that filled the court as an accompaniment to Costecalde's tears, the three big-wigs were seen for a moment to confer together.

Then his Honor addressed the witness:

"You say Rugimabaud was eaten up by a shark before your eyes? But the Court has just been hearing as witness for the prosecution a certain Rugimabaud who arrived here this morning; may he not be by chance the same person as the hero of your anecdote?"

"Yes, indeed—rather! I *am* the same, it's me!" roared the ex-Commissioner of Agriculture.

"Bless me, Rugimabaud is here?" exclaimed Costecalde, not in the least disconcerted. "I didn't see him—it's the first I've heard of him."

"He wasn't eaten up by a shark, then, as you've just described?"

"I think I must have confounded him with Truphénus."

"Oh, I say, *I'm* here!" protested Truphénus in turn.

"At any rate, be it one or be it the other, what I know is that somebody or other was eaten by a shark!"

And with the utmost calmness Costecalde continued to answer questions as if nothing had occurred.

Before he stepped down, one of the judges desired to know, by his estimate, the exact number of victims, of one kind and another.

"Forty thousand!"

He rolled so the r's of his "for-r-ty," that, as if for the pleasure of hearing him do it again, the judge exclaimed:

"How is that? How many?"

"Forty thousand!"

"You say forty thousand?"

"At the very least, your Honor."

Now, the records of the colony were there to attest that at no moment whatever had there been on the island more than four hundred Tarasconians.

Confronted with this kind of evidence, the bewilderment of his Honor could only grow. It was shared by his august colleagues, now completely awake, who perspired with amazement as much as with heat, never having been present at such a trial as this, and thinking that every one concerned in it must be simply mad. There was nothing but violent interruptions and flat contradictions, which increased as the row of witnesses grew longer, all jumping up and down, gesticulating, talking at once, snatching the words out of each others' mouths. A preposterous trial indeed, a tragi-comedy exclusively consisting of people eaten, drowned, cooked, roasted, boiled, devoured, tattooed, who yet had turned up there together in the same row, all in perfect health and with their full complement of limbs.

In regard to the few who had not answered to the roll, you couldn't say they were really dead any more than the others, that they wouldn't rise again the next minute like their friends; which is the reason why M. Bonicar, the magistrate, more intimately versed in the nature of his countrymen, had recommended Monsieur Mouillard to leave out the question of manslaughter through criminal neglect.

The unhappy Mouillard, submerged in the rising flood of contradictory evidence, demanded silence without getting it, and had repeatedly to threaten to clear the court. The spectators, in their zeal for one side or the other, paid not the least attention to him; so that, giving it all up, he leaned his elbows on his desk and held his head with his hands as if it would burst.

During a short comparative lull, M. Roger du Nord, a little old man with long white whiskers and a sarcastic smile, who was not without wit, said aloud, bending over, with his judge's cap a little askew:

"In short, in the lot, it seems to me that the only thing that has not come back is the Tarasque."

At this M. Bompard du Mazet, the Public Prosecutor, sprang up with a movement of a jack-in-the-box:

"And my uncle, then?"

"And Bravida, then?" cried Costecalde.

The Public Prosecutor went on with high dignity but rising emotion:

"I beg the Court to observe that my unfortunate uncle was one of the earliest victims. If I have had the discretion not to speak of him in my indictment, it's none the less true that this particular absentee has not come back, and will never come back."

"I beg your pardon, Mr. Prosecutor," interrupted the principal worthy on the bench; "it so happens that your uncle at this very moment sends in his card to me and requests to be heard."

This piece of news produced an immense rumpus. The public, the witnesses, the accused, all sprang to their feet, scrambled upon the seats, waved their arms, shouted, and exhibited astonishment and curiosity in the good Tarasconian fashion; while his Honor, to restore order, directed the Court to rise for a few moments, of which advantage was taken to remove two or three constables who had fainted, and were half dead with heat and mystification.

V.

"'It's he—it's Gonzago! I say—did you ever?'
'Bless us, how he has filled out!'
'Mercy, how he has bleached!'
'You'd take him for a Turk!'"

THE crowd stretched forward, agape, so long had honest Bompard been removed from its ken. He had been tremendously lean of old, dry, brown, and mustachioed like a Greek brigand, with the eyes of a crazy goat; but now he was well rounded out, though showing in his big puffed face the same swaggering mustache and the same nonsensical eyes.

Looking neither to right nor to left, he followed the usher into the witness-box, where Monsieur Mouillard began to examine him.

"There's no doubt about your identity, Gonzague Bompard?"

"To tell the truth, your Honor, I almost doubt of it myself when I see"—here he let off a noble gesture in the direction of the accused

—"when I see, I say, our purest glory on that bench of infamy, and when, within these walls, I hear insult heaped upon the soul of honor and probity!"

"Oh, thanks, Gonzago!" cried Tartarin from his place, suffocated with emotion.

He had borne without wincing every calumny, but the sympathy of his old comrade made his heart burst, filled his eyes with the tears of a pitied child.

"Yes, yes, my gallant friend," Bompard went on, "you won't remain there long on your filthy bench. I bring with me the proof—the proof "

He fumbled in his pockets, drew out a clay pipe, a knife, an old flint, a match-box, a piece of string, a yard-measure, and a little case of homœopathic medicines; all of which objects he laid one after the other on the table of the clerk of the court.

"Come, Mr. Bompard," said his Honor, out of patience; "just mention it when you've done."

"I say, uncle, hurry up a bit," added M. Bompard du Mazet.

His uncle turned towards him.

"Ah yes, you'd better meddle, you wretch, after the beautiful line you have taken! Treating our dear old friend as a swindler! Just wait till I get round there and cut you off with a shilling, little scoundrel!"

The nephew kept sufficiently cool under this threat, and the uncle, continuing to fumble and

arranging before him a whole museum of fantastic objects, found at last what he sought.

"Here, your Honor, is a letter which makes it as plain as day that the so-called Duc de Mons is the biggest villain on earth, a regular vagabond and gallows-bird, the only guilty one, the only one who ought to be laden with chains, and on the bench of infamy."

"That will do—give me the letter."

Monsieur Mouillard took the letter, read it, and passed it to his two colleagues, who in turn began to examine it, and turn it upsidedown and inside out. During this examination the faces of the three judges remained inscrutable and impenetrable. You could see they were real judges of the North. Staring at their inexpressive masks, it was very hard for the public to get an idea of what the mysterious letter contained; the only thing that could be gathered was the extreme importance of the document.

Every one stood on tiptoe; some screwed round their heads as if to get a look; the hubbub of voices increased, the wave of curiosity broke in the depths of the gallery.

"What is it, what's in it, what is it all about?"

And the agitation in the court gaining the crowd outside, to which the successive phases of the case were communicated through the open windows and doors, there rose an uproar on the Long Walk, a confusion and a clamor like the surge of the sea in a stiff breeze.

The good constables accordingly waked up, the flies forsook the ceiling and began to buzz about; the waning afternoon brought with it a few wandering airs, so that, as the Tarasconians dread nothing so much as a draught, the spectators who were near the windows began to shout for them to be closed—they were afraid of "catching their death."

For the hundredth time the unhappy Mouillard bawled, "Silence, silence for a moment, or I clear the court!" Then he continued the examination.

Question. "Witness Bompard, how and when did this letter come into your hands?"

Answer. "When the *Farandole* was starting from Marseilles the duke, or so-called duke, handed me my papers as Provisional Governor of the settlement, and at the same time he slipped into my palm this big letter, fastened, though it contained no money, with eight red seals. He told me I should find in it his very last instructions, and he directed me particularly not to open it till we should reach some islands or other—the Admiralty Isles—in the 144th degree of longitude. It's marked there on the envelope—you can see."

Q. "Yes, yes; I see. And then?"

A. "Then, your Honor, you see, I was suddenly taken awfully ill, as you must have been told; it seemed to be a sort of catching thing, so that, although I felt near my end, they put me ashore at the Chateau d'If. Once ashore, I was doubled up with pain; but the letter was in my pocket, for in my agony I had forgotten to give it to Bézuquet when I handed him over my credentials."

Q. "It is a pity you forgot. Well, then?"

A. "Well, then, your Honor, when I got a little better and was able to get up and put on my clothes again—it was a good bit later, a long time—one day I happened to put my hand in my pocket by chance, and, lo and behold! there was the blessed letter with the red seals!"

Here Monsieur Mouillard interrupted the witness with great severity:

"Witness Bompard, would it not be more conformable to truth to say that this letter, destined to be unsealed only four thousand leagues away from France, was by preference opened by your hand on the spot, on the very deck of the ship, so that you might see what was in it, whereupon, acquainted with its contents, you shrank from the immense responsibilities it entailed upon you?"

"You don't know Bompard, your Honor," this

personage replied. "I appeal to all Tarascon, present in this court."

The silence of the tomb greeted this oratorical flight. Enjoying on the lips of his fellow-citizens the sobriquet of the Impostor, Bompard, perhaps, went a little far in calling on them to back him up. Tarascon sounded, therefore, gave back no echo, which, however, did not prevent the speaker from going on imperturbably:

"Your Honor sees, silence, as the proverb says, means consent." And continuing his story: "When it came to that, when I found the letter, Bézuquet, who had left so many weeks before, was too far away for me to overtake him; so that I made up my mind to see what *was* in the confounded thing. Acting upon this, imagine my horrible situation!"

A horrible situation, most horrible, too, was that of the audience, still perfectly ignorant of the contents of the precious document under discussion, tormentingly fingered by the judges.

It was vain to crane over, it was vain to stretch and stare; the coveted knowledge was out of reach—nothing was visible but the big red seals of the wrapper.

"What was I to do, miserable me," Bompard went on, "after I had read such horrors? Was I to strike out and try to swim after the ship?

Alas, it was beyond my strength. Was I, by making public my abominable missive, to prevent the *Tootoopumpum* from sailing? Was I to dash with cold water the enthusiasm of the panting remnant of our party? They would have risen in their wrath and stoned me! I was in such a dreadful dilemma that I was afraid to show myself at Tarascon. At last I made up my mind to go and hide over opposite, at Beaucaire, where I should be able to see everything without being seen. I succeeded in obtaining simultaneous possession of two offices there—that of Warden of the Fair-grounds and that of Conservator of the Castle. I had a certain amount of leisure, as you may believe, and from the top of the old tower, with a good glass, I watched on the other side of the Rhone the agitation of my unhappy compatriots, all bustling for departure. And I gnawed my heart, I wrung my hands, I held out my arms to them, bawling to them from afar, as if they might have heard me: 'Stop, stop—stay, stay—don't go—turn round and go home!' I even tried to warn them back by means of a bottle. Tell his Honor, Tartarin, tell him that I tried to warn you."

"Yes, it's true," said Tartarin from the bench of infamy.

"Ah, your Honor, what I suffered when I saw

the *Tootoopumpum* really set sail for the land of dreams! But I suffered still more when they all came back and when I learned that, opposite to me there, the greatest of my countrymen was languishing in fetters. To know that he was immured in that dungeon and under a false charge—it was really too much. You will tell me that I ought to have produced the proof of his innocence sooner; but when once one is started on the wrong road it's the deuce and all to get back to the right one. I began by saying nothing, and it had become more and more difficult to speak at last. Then you don't count the Bridge, the dreadful Bridge that I should have had to cross again! So long as the preliminary inquiry lasted I hoped the whole thing would be quashed; but when I saw that you were really going on, knew that Tartarin was really dragged into the dock between the myrmidons of the law, then I could hold out no longer, I let myself go—I crossed the Bridge. I crossed it this morning in a terrible tempest; I was obliged to go down on all fours, the same way as when I went up Mont Blanc. You remember that, Tartarin?"

"Remember it?" Tartarin rumbled.

"When I tell you that the Bridge was swinging like a pendulum you'll believe I had to be

brave. I was, in fact, heroic. But here I am, at any rate, and this time I bring you the proof, the irrefutable proof."

Of the irrefutability of the proof neither of the three gentlemen on the bench seemed particularly convinced; and the senior, in his cold, calm voice, expressed their common doubts.

"Who guarantees that this strange letter, buried so long in your pocket, is really by the person De Mons? You see, we have to leave a margin, with all you good people. Such a flood of lies as I've been listening to for three hours!"

A long murmur rolled through the room, surged in the galleries.

Tarascon hardly liked this—Tarascon protested. As for Bompard, he answered simply with a smile:

"So far as I'm concerned, your Honor, I won't absolutely claim that I'm the most literal creature in the world—no, I won't go so far as that. But see here; just ask a question or two of my friend there." And he waved his hand at Tartarin. "In the way of the literal, he's about the best thing we have here."

"Usher, hand this letter to the accused," said the judge.

Tartarin took it, examined it, declared that he recognized the handwriting and the signature unfortunately too familiar to him; then, still erect, turning towards the bench, with a light in his eye, a ring in his voice, and the famous letter brandished in his hand: "In my turn, your Honor, armed with this cynical lucubration, I summon you to acknowledge that all the impostors don't come from the South. Ah, you call us liars, us poor performers of Tarascon! But we are only people of imagination and of overflowing speech—people who hit it off, people who embroider, people whose fertile fancy throws off things on the spur of the moment, and who are themselves the first to be taken in, even when they are surprised, by their own ingenuous readiness. How different from your liars of the North—deliberate, elaborate, and perverse, with their rascally practical machinations—such a one, for instance, as the signer of this letter! Yes, thank God, one may say that in the way of lying, when the North tries its hand the South is no match for it at all!"

Launched on this theme, with his good-sense and eloquence, Tartarin ought to have raised the house. But it was all over. The great man had decidedly forfeited public favor. No one had an ear for him. Exasperated curiosity had no ear and no eye for anything but the mysterious missive with eight red seals that he waved up and down in his hand.

Devil take it! what *could* there be in this tantalizing scroll which they handed to and fro without coming to the point and reading it out?

Tartarin would have liked to go on, but the

impatience of his fellow-citizens gave him no chance. They only shouted from all sides, "The letter—the letter! Read us the letter!"

Monsieur Mouillard again threatened to clear the court if they didn't keep quiet; but at last, yielding to the popular desire, and addressing the accused:

"So I am to take it from you that this is really the writing of the person De Mons?"

"You may take it from me. The hands are identical, your Honor."

"Hand the letter to the clerk of the court, so that he may read it out."

A huge "Ah!" of relief greeted these words, and was followed by a silence so deep that you could hear nothing but the buzz of the flies within and the shrill of the insects without. Every one sat motionless in his place, cocking his head to one side to hear better.

Amid this solemn attention of a whole people the clerk of the court, in a slow, monotonous, nasal voice, began to read the letter with the eight red seals:

"*To Mr. Gonzago Bompard, Provisional Governor of the Colony of Port Tarascon: to be opened in* 144° 30′ *longitude east, opposite the Admiralty Isles.*

"MY DEAR MONSIEUR BOMPARD,—There is no joke good enough to be kept up forever.

Put straight about and come quietly back with your Tarasconians.

"There is no island, there is no treaty, there is no Port Tarascon; there are no acres nor concessions nor distilleries nor refineries, there is nothing of any kind. Nothing, at least, but a splendid operation by which I have pocketed some millions, which are now, I am happy to say, in as safe a place as my person.

"What it has all come to is a nice little Tarasconade, which your fellow-citizens and illustrious chief will certainly forgive me, since it has afforded them occupation and recreation, and revived their taste, which they had rather lost, for their delicious little town.

"Duc De Mons.

"P. S.—No more a duke than Mons is his duchy. Scarcely known in the neighborhood."

Ah, this time his lordship could only threaten in vain to clear the court; nothing could restrain the roars, the yells, the howls of rage that broke forth and reached the street, the Long Walk, the Esplanade, resounded through the

whole town. Ah, the Belgian, the dirty Belgian; how they would have chucked him into the Rhone if they could only have got hold of him!

Every one lent his voice—men, women, and children—and it was in the midst of this appalling din, the racket of an angry hive, that Monsieur Mouillard pronounced the acquittal of Tartarin and of Pascalon, to the great despair of Cicero Franquebalme, who was obliged to keep to himself his great speech, to pack up again the solid blocks of his argument, all his whatsoevers and whensoevers and wheresoevers—to swallow, in a word, his masterpiece, his compact, cemented Roman aqueduct.

The public poured forth from the court, spread over the town, surged through the Walk Round, through the squares and bits of squares, continuing to relieve itself in wild vociferations. Ah, the Belgian, the dirty Belgian! his name was everywhere mingled with the cry that has ever since remained the bloodiest insult that a Tarasconian can utter, "Liar of the North!—liar of the North!"

VI.

October 8th.—Resumed my position in Ferdinand Bézuquet's pharmacy. I have regained the esteem of my countrymen and recovered the tranquillity of my former existence on the bit of a square between the two jars, the yellow and the green, of the shop-front. There is only this difference, that poor Bézuquet now sticks fast to the back shop, as if he were the apprentice, where he works the pestle from morning to night, pounding his drugs in the marble mortar in a kind of rage, as if he hoped they would feel it! He only stops from time to time to take a little mirror out of his pocket and look at his tattooings. Poor Ferdinand! neither poultice nor plaster can touch them; there is no help for him even in the nice little garlic broth recommended by Dr. Tournatoire. He has got them for life, his infernal illuminations.

Meanwhile I put up little parcels, I write little labels, I exchange little remarks with little customers, and I find a sufficient amusement in the little gossip of the little town. On market-days we have always a lot of people. Since the wine-crop shows signs of mending, our peasants have begun again to dose and drug themselves; in the country about Tarascon there is no more cherished pursuit. On Tuesday and Friday the pharmacy is crammed.

The rest of the week it is sufficiently quiet; the shop bell tinkles less frequently. I pass my time in looking at the superscriptions of the great glass bottles and the great jars of white earthen-ware ranged on the shelves—the *sirupus gummi*, the *assafœtida*, and the φαρμα κοπούα, in Greek characters, between two serpents over the counter.

After so many agitations and adventures, this lull in my existence is rather enjoyable. I am preparing a volume of verses in our dear old dialect: *Li Ginjourlo* (" Drops of Jujube "). In the North the jujube is known only as a pharmaceutic product, but here the tree, with its thin foliage, produces a different fruit, a kind of charming little red olive that melts in your mouth. I shall collect in this volume my little landscapes and my love-poems.

Woe is me! I sometimes see her pass, my long and flexible Clorinda, skipping over the sharp cobble-stones of the bit of a square with the same motion that on the island we used to compare to that of the kangaroo. She's going to second mass, her prayer-book in her hand, followed by the valuable female domestic who used to patch up our roofs and "shin" up our flag-staffs, and who, since our return to Tarascon, has passed from the service of Mademoiselle Tournatoire to that of the marquise and her daughter. Never once has the high-born damsel cast a glance at our poor shop. From the moment I crossed its threshold again I ceased to exist for her.

The town has recovered its ancient tranquillity, and seems quite at home again. We stroll on the Long Walk and on the Esplanade; in the evening we go to the club and to the play. Every one has come back except Brother Bataillet, who stopped over in the Philippines to set up a new community of White Fathers. Here the convent of Pampérigouste has opened its doors a little—just on a crack—and the Reverend Father Vezole (God be praised!) is settled in it again with a few other holy men. The bells have begun to tinkle gently, ever so gently.

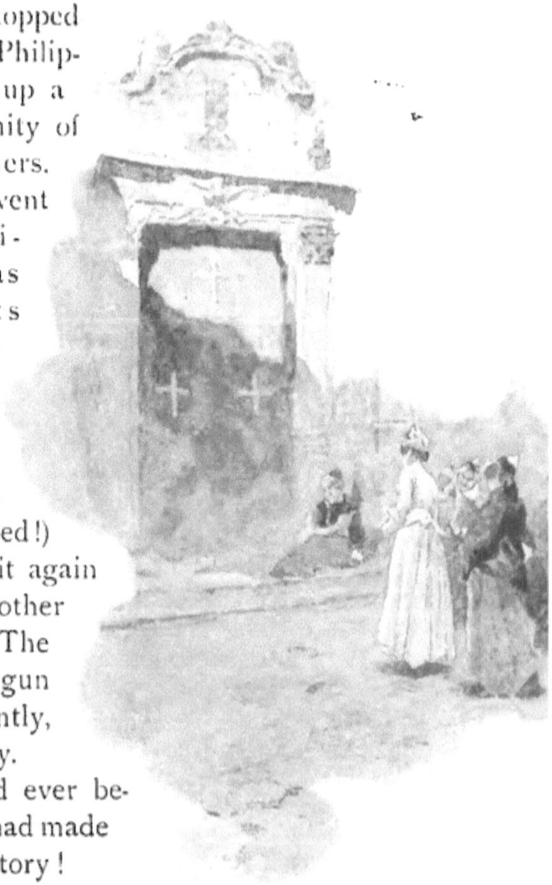

Who would ever believe that we had made so much history!

How far it all seems now, and what rare fellows we are to forget! To appreciate this you must see our sportsmen, the Marquis des Espazettes at their head, start out every Sunday morning, in brand-new trappings, to shoot game that doesn't exist.

On my side, on Sunday, after breakfast, I go and pay my respects to Tartarin. It is there still, at the end of the Long Walk, the little house with the green blinds; the little boot-blacks are there still before the gate, but somehow they are stricken with silence, and everything is lifeless and closed. I lift the latch, and passing in, I find the hero in his garden, turning round the tank of goldfish, with his hands behind him, or else in his study, surrounded by his poisoned arrows and other outlandish weapons. At present he never even looks at his beloved collections. The setting is the same, but how the man has changed! It was fruitless for them to let him off; they couldn't give him back his honor, they couldn't give him back his glory. The great man feels that that glory has waned—this is the secret of his sadness.

But we talk together, and sometimes Dr. Tournatoire comes in, bringing to the melancholy house his good-humor and his somewhat primitive, his even questionable, medical jokes.

Franquebalme also comes on Sunday, Tartarin having confided to him the protection of his interests. He has a lawsuit at Toulon with Captain Scrapouchinat, who is trying to recover from him the expenses of the return trip; another suit, too, with the widow of Bravida, who has brought it as the guardian of her bereaved children. If my poor dear master loses either of these cases, how in the world will he keep afloat? He has already sunk most of his substance in the lamentable adventure of Port Tarascon.

Would to Heaven I were rich! Unfortunately the money I get from Bézuquet isn't the sort of thing to enable me to assist my noble friend.

October 10th.—My "Jujubes" are to appear at Avignon, with the imprint of Roumanille. I'm awfully happy about it. Another piece of good-luck is that they are getting up a great procession in honor of St. Martha, whose feast is on the 19th, and in honor, too, of the restoration of our race to the soil of France. Dourladoure and I, perched on an allegorical car, are to represent Provençal poetry.

October 20th.—Yesterday, Sunday, our procession came off. A long stream of cars and cavaliers, the latter in historical costumes, holding out on long wands butterfly-nets for money. A tremendous crowd of people, a cluster of heads at every window, and yet, in spite of everything, a visible want of real animation. The ingenious managers of the fête had vainly endeavored to make up for the absence of our dear Old Granny; every one was conscious of a gap, of a void—the car of the Tarasque was not there. Smothered rancor woke up again at the thought of the dastardly shot discharged in the far Pacific; as we passed before Tartarin's house the mutter of resentment might have been heard in the ranks. As at this moment Costecalde's ill-conditioned gang tried to work up the crowd, the Marquis des Espazettes, who was dressed as a Templar, turned round on his horse—"Quiet there, you know, gentlemen!" He had quite the grand air, and the disorder was instantly checked.

The *tramontana* was blowing, and there was unmistakable snow in it, as Dourladoure and I were cruelly conscious in our picturesque habits. We had borrowed our dresses—of the period of Charles VI.—from the opera-troupe that happens to be here now; and seated, each of us, on the battlements of a tower (for our chariot, drawn by six white oxen, was supposed to represent King René's castle, in wood and painted pasteboard), we were pierced through and through by the rascally blast, so that the verses we recited to our big lyres chattered as much as the speakers. Dourladoure remarked to me that we were simply freezing. But we had to freeze, we couldn't get down, for want of ladders, those on which we had clambered up having been inconsiderately removed.

On the Walk Round our sufferings were more than we could bear; and, to finish them up, what did I do but bethink myself—oh, vanity of love!—to take a short-cut and pass directly in front of the residence of a certain high-born family.

So behold us squeezed into the narrow streets of that part, with only just room for the wheels of the car. The noble mansion was shut up, dark and dumb behind the black stones of its old walls, with all its shutters drawn, to show how the aristocracy sniffs at the pleasures of the Rabble-babble.

I repeated a few lines, in my quavering voice, and

poked out my little bag to beg; but nothing stirred—no one appeared. Then I ordered the driver to move on. But it was impossible, the car was stuck, wedged in—it was vain to pull it from its front or to drag it from behind; it was simply held fast between the high walls. Close to us, between the slits of the shutters, on a level with our ears, we heard a smothered giggle; in the face of which we had to stay ridiculously perched on our pasteboard turrets, numb with cold in spite of our burning shame.

Decidedly, King René's castle didn't bring me much luck. The oxen had to be taken out and ladders to be brought to get us down—all of which seemed interminable!

October 28th.—What is it, then, what can it be, the ache for glory? It is clear that when once one has known it one can't live without it.

Last Sunday I called on Tartarin, and we talked together in the garden, strolling along the sanded paths. Over the wall the trees on the Long Walk scattered their leaves down in heaps, and as I noticed the melancholy in his eyes, I tried to remind him of the glorious hours of his life. But nothing could bring him round, not even the various similitudes between his career and Napoleon's.

"Oh, don't humbug me with your Napoleon!

When I fell into that the sun of the tropics had muddled my brain. Don't ever talk of it again, please: I shall be obliged to you."

I looked at him in stupefaction.

"Well, but my dear friend, the Commodore's lady—"

"Leave me alone with your Commodore's lady—the Commodore's lady was making a fool of me!"

We took a few more steps in silence, while an occasional cry from one of the little boot-blacks (they were playing jack-stones on the other side of the wall) mingled with the gusts that whirled the dry leaves. Tartarin added, in a moment:

"I see through it now; the Tarasconians have opened my eyes. It is as if I had been operated on for cataract."

He struck me as extraordinary.

Later, when I was going, he suddenly said, as I pressed his hand: "Do you know, my dear child, I'm going to have a sale? I've lost my suit against Scrapouchinat, and the other one against Madame Bravida as well, for all the dialectics of Franquebalme. The fellow builds too big; it tumbles down on top of you, and buries you beneath its weight."

Ever so timidly I offered him my little savings. I would have given them to him with all my heart, but Tartarin wouldn't listen to it.

"Thank you, my child; I dare say my arms, my curiosities, my rare plants, will bring in enough. If it's not enough I'll sell the house. After that we shall see. Farewell, dear child: these things are nothing!"

Dear me, what philosophy!

October 31st.—To-day I've had a great sorrow. I was in the shop, serving Madame Truphénus with a remedy for her baby, who has measles, when a creak of wheels on the bit of a square made me raise my head. I had recog-

nized the sound of the springs of the great coach of the old Dowager of Aigueboulide. The old woman was inside, with her stuffed parrot beside her, and opposite sat my Clorinda, with another person whom I couldn't see very well, as the sun was in my eyes—a person in a blue uniform and an embroidered military cap.

"Who in the world is with those ladies?"

"Why, the dowager's grandson, Vicomte Charlexis d'Aigueboulide, an officer in the light cavalry. Didn't you know that Miss Clorinda and he are to be 'married together' this very next month?"

It gave me a blow. I must have looked like a corpse.

After all, I had still had a hope.

"Oh, you know, it's quite one of your love-matches," continued my clumsy customer. "But do you know what we say?—

"'When you marry to your taste,
Your nights and days you're sure to waste.'"

Lackaday! that's the way I should have liked to marry.

November 5th.—Yesterday poor Tartarin's auction came off. I was not there, but Franquebalme came to the shop in the evening and told me all about it.

It seems to have been heart-rending. The sale hasn't brought a penny. It took place outside, before the door, according to our old custom. Literally, not a penny, and yet there were a lot of people. The arms of all countries—the poisoned arrows, the assegais, the yataghans, the revolvers, the Winchester, the thirty-two shooter—not a single sou did they fetch. The same with the splendid lion-skins of the Atlas; the same with the great alpenstock, his glorious staff of the Jungfrau; there was only here and there a preposterous bid for these curiosities, these treasures—the real museum of our city. Yes, faith is dead.

And then the baobab in its little pot—the wondrous exotic that for thirty years has been the admiration of the country! When it was placed on the table, when the auctioneer described it as "*Arbos gigantea*—whole villages are often covered by its shade"—it seems there was a universal guffaw.

Tartarin heard this profane mirth from the other side of the wall—he was taking a turn or two in his little garden with a couple of friends. He said to them, without bitterness:

"They, too, our good Tarasconians, have been through the operation for cataract. Yes, now they can see; but they're cruel."

The saddest thing of all is that the sale is far from having produced enough to clear off his debts. He has been obliged to dispose of his house to the Espazettes, who mean to give it to their young couple.

And he, the poor great man, what will become

of him? Will he cross the Bridge, as has been vaguely stated? Will he take refuge at Beaucaire with his old friend Bompard?

While Franquebalme, standing in the middle of the shop, dwelt on this dismal episode, Bézuquet, in the background, just peeping, with his ineffaceable blazonry, through a gap in the door, tossed us, with the laugh of a Papuan fiend, a "Serves him right! serves him right!" as if it were Tartarin himself who had tattooed him!

November 7th.—It is to-morrow, Sunday, that my kind master is to leave the city and cross the Bridge! Can it be possible? Is Tartarin of Tarascon to become Tartarin of Beaucaire? Just see what a difference, if only to the ear! And then the Bridge, the terrible Bridge to cross. I know very well that Tartarin has run other risks, and surmounted other obstacles; but, all the same, those are things that you say in anger—you don't really do them. I can't believe it yet.

Sunday, December 10th.—Seven o'clock in the evening. I've come in quite prostrate—I've hardly strength to jot down these words.

It's done; he's gone; he has crossed the Bridge!

Three or four of us had agreed to meet at his house; there were Tournatoire and Franquebalme and Beaumevieille, and we were overtaken on the way by Malbos, one of the veterans of the militia.

My heart sank dreadfully at the sight of the wretched bare walls and the ravaged garden; but Tartarin didn't even look round him.

That's the good side of our Tarasconian nature—our incurable mobility. It helps us to be less sad than other races.

He gave the keys to Franquebalme.

"You will hand them to the Marquis des Espazettes. I bear him no grudge for not having come; it's quite natural. As Bravida used to say:

"'The love of the great
Is brittle friendship.
As soon as they've done with us
They turn their backs.'"

Turning to me, he added, "You know something about that, dear child."

This allusion to Clorinda touched me. To think of *me* in such a peck of troubles!

When once we had got out on the Long Walk we found it was blowing fearfully. Each of us thought to himself, "Mercy on us! look out for the Bridge presently."

Tartarin didn't seem to be looking out for it at all. The mistral had blown every one out of the streets; we met nothing but the garrison band coming back from the Esplanade, the soldiers, bothered with their instruments, holding fast with the other hand their capes, that were flapping and flying away.

Tartarin talked slowly, strolling between us as if he were taking the air. He talked about himself.

"You see, the trouble with me has been that I have had, in an extraordinary degree, the affection we all have. I've fed myself too much on *regardelle*."

At Tarascon we call *regardelle* everything that tempts desire, everything we long for and yet can't put our hand upon. It is the food of the dreamer—of imaginative people. And Tartarin told the truth—nobody has eaten more *regardelle* than he.

As I was carrying my hero's valise and bandbox, as well as his overcoat, I walked a little behind and didn't catch everything. Some of his words were blown away in the wind—it blew ever so much stronger as we approached the Rhone. I gathered that he was saying he bore nobody a grudge, talking of his career with genial philosophy.

"That ragamuffin of a Daudet has said somewhere that I'm Don Quixote in the skin of

Sancho Panza. Well, I suppose it's true. This type of the fat Don Quixote, the Don Quixote comfortably potted in his flesh, and always falling below his dream, is rather frequent at Tarascon and its neighborhood."

A little farther, down a side street, we saw capering along a back that we recognized. It was Escourbaniès, crying, "A lot of noise! let's make a lot of noise! long life to Costecalde!" as he passed the shop-front of the armorer, who, as it happens, was this morning appointed a municipal councillor.

"I've not the slightest feeling even against *him*," said Tartarin. "And yet such a fellow as that represents the most horrible side of our Tarasconian South. I don't speak of his everlasting chatter, though he really chatters more than is necessary, but of that dreadful desire to please, to be amiable, which makes him do the vilest and most abject things. He's with Costecalde to throw me into the Rhone. He would be with me, if any good were to be got by it, to do the same for Costecalde. But except for that, my children, we are not so bad; it's a nice little race, without which, long ago, our poor old France would have died of pedantry and *ennui*."

We had reached the river. Before us hung

a wild sunset, a few clouds high in the air. The wind seemed to have fallen a little, but all the same the Bridge was not tempting. We stopped at this end of it; he didn't ask us to go farther.

"Well, then, my dears, farewell!"

He embraced us all, beginning with Beaumevieille, as the oldest, and ending with me. I was wet, I was perfectly dripping with tears,

which I couldn't wipe, encumbered as I was with his portmanteau and overcoat, so that I may say the great man literally drank them up.

Deeply moved himself, he took over his property, the bandbox in one hand, the great-coat over the arm, the valise in the other hand. At last Tournatoire said to him:

"Above all, Tartarin, take good care of yourself—you know the climate over there, the mortality at Beaucaire! A little garlic broth—don't forget that!"

Our friend replied, with a wink:

"Don't be afraid; you know the old woman's account of herself, 'the farther she went the more she learned, and the less she wanted to die.' I shall be like the old woman."

We saw him pass from us under the cables, a little heavy but with a good step. The Bridge was lurching horribly. Two or three times he stopped to catch his hat, which was blowing away, and we cried to him from the distance, but without budging:

"Farewell, Tartarin—farewell!"

He never turned round. He answered nothing; his feelings were too much for him. He only joggled his bandbox up and down behind him as a response.

Three months later, one Sunday evening.—I've

opened my *Memorial* again after a long interval—this old green diary that I mean to leave to my children, if I ever have any, worn at the corners, begun five thousand leagues from home, the companion of my vicissitudes at sea, in prison, everywhere. There's a little room in it still, of which I take advantage to enter a report that has been in circulation since this morning—the rumor that Tartarin has ceased to be!

For three months we have had no news of him. I have known that he had settled at Beaucaire, in company with Bompard, whom he has been helping to superintend the Fair-grounds and watch over the Castle. Such occupations come back, after all, to the old *regardelle*. I have pined for my kind master so often that I have had twenty minds to go and see him, but I have always been kept back by that fiend of a Bridge.

One day, looking over towards the Castle of Beaucaire, it seemed to me that I saw somebody perched upon it with an opera-glass directed this way. The figure looked as if it might be Bompard. He disappeared, went back into the tower, and presently returned with a companion, a very stout party, who had a look of Tartarin. This companion also took the glass, but lowered it presently to wave his arms as a sort of sign; the thing, however, was so far off and slight and sketchy that I was not quite so much excited by it as I ought to have been.

This morning when I got up I felt awfully

uneasy, but without knowing why. I went out to the barber's, as I do every Sunday, and was struck with the curious, muffled, sallow sky, one of those thick, dead skies that make the trees

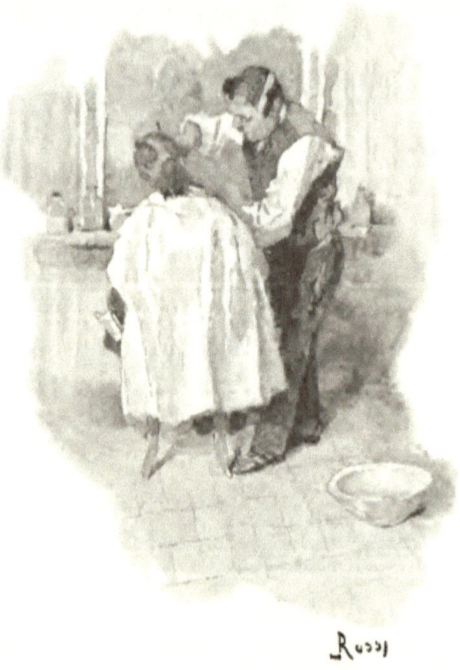

and branches, the pavements and houses, so strangely distinct. When I reached the barber's—I always go to Marc Aurèle—I called his attention to it.

"What a funny sun! It doesn't warm, it doesn't light! Is there an eclipse coming off?"

"Why, don't you know about it, Monsieur Pascalon? They've been expecting one since the beginning of the month."

And at the moment he had got hold of my nose, and had his razor just under it.

"And the news—I suppose you know the news, eh? It appears our great man is no longer of this world."

"What great man?"

When he named Tartarin I only wanted a little of making him cut my throat.

"That's what it is to leave home! Without Tarascon he couldn't live."

My friend Marcus Aurelius didn't know he was so near the truth.

Without Tarascon and without glory it was very certain Tartarin couldn't live.

My kind old master—my dear great friend!

The coincidence is awfully striking—an eclipse the day of his death!

What a funny people we are, after all! I'll bet anything that there's not a creature in town who isn't saddened by the news, which, however, won't prevent every one from trying to look as much as possible as if he didn't mind it.

All this because, ever since we made such fools of ourselves out there, showing ourselves so hoaxing and so hoaxed, we have all wanted to take the other line and appear to have learned, once for all, the lesson of steadiness and sobriety.

The truth is, however, that we've not learned any lesson at all; only now instead of saying too much about anything we say too little—we lie by understatement.

We no longer say that yesterday, in our old arena, there were at least fifty thousand people; we say it's putting it strong to call them at the very most half a dozen.

It's only another kind exaggeration!

THE ODD NUMBER SERIES.

MODERN GHOSTS. Selected and translated from the Works of GUY DE MAUPASSANT, PEDRO ANTONIO DE ALARCÓN, and Others. An Introduction by GEORGE WILLIAM CURTIS. 16mo, Cloth, Ornamental, $1 00.

THE HOUSE BY THE MEDLAR-TREE. By GIOVANNI VERGA. Translated from the Italian by MARY A. CRAIG. An Introduction by W. D. HOWELLS. 16mo, Cloth, Ornamental, $1 00.

Almost beyond question one of the cleverest and truest of modern novels.—*N. Y. Tribune.*

PASTELS IN PROSE. (From the French.) Translated by STUART MERRILL. With 150 Illustrations (including Frontispiece in Color) by H. W. McVICKAR, and Introduction by W. D. HOWELLS. pp. xvi., 270. 16mo, Cloth, Ornamental, $1 25.

No greater compliment can be paid the translator than the wholly truthful remark that one forgets in the reading that any other words than those of his choosing have ever clothed these rare and lovely fancies.—*Boston Transcript.*

MARÍA: A SOUTH AMERICAN ROMANCE. By JORGE ISAACS. Translated by ROLLO OGDEN. An Introduction by THOMAS A. JANVIER. pp. xvi., 302. 16mo, Cloth, Ornamental, $1 00.

A beautiful story, beautifully told; and so admirable does the translation seem to be that the reader is unconscious of a single alien note. —*Academy*, London.

THE ODD NUMBER: Thirteen Tales by GUY DE MAUPASSANT. The Translation by JONATHAN STURGES. An Introduction by HENRY JAMES. pp. xviii., 226. 16mo, Cloth, Ornamental, $1 00.

M. Guy de Maupassant is seen at his best in this baker's dozen of short stories. Judged by conciseness and readiness of expression, they are an array of masterpieces.—*Philadelphia Ledger.*

BY CHAS. DUDLEY WARNER.

A LITTLE JOURNEY IN THE WORLD. A Novel. pp. iv., 396. Post 8vo, Half Leather, Uncut Edges and Gilt Top, $1 50.

"A Little Journey in the World" has all the best qualities of Mr. Warner's style, and is brimful of wit, humor, and satire.—*Independent*, N. Y.

One of the brightest novels of contemporary American life.—*N. Y. Journal of Commerce*.

A powerful picture of that phase of modern life in which unscrupulously acquired capital is the chief agent. . . . Mr. Warner has depicted this phase of society with real power, and there are passages in his work which are a nearer approach to Thackeray than we have had from any American author.—*Boston Post*.

STUDIES IN THE SOUTH AND WEST, with Comments on Canada. pp. iv., 484. Post 8vo, Half Leather, Uncut Edges and Gilt Top, $1 75.

Sketches made from studies of the country and the people upon the ground. . . . They are the opinions of a man and a scholar without prejudices, and only anxious to state the facts as they were. . . When told in the pleasant and instructive way of Mr. Warner the studies are as delightful as they are instructive.—*Chicago Inter-Ocean*.

Perhaps the most accurate and graphic account of these portions of the country that has appeared, taking all in all. . . . It is a book most charming—a book that no American can fail to enjoy, appreciate, and highly prize.—*Boston Traveller*.

THEIR PILGRIMAGE. Richly Illustrated by C. S. REINHART. pp. viii., 364. Post 8vo, Half Leather, Uncut Edges and Gilt Top, $2 00.

Mr. Warner's pen-pictures of the characters typical of each resort, of the manner of life followed at each, of the humor and absurdities peculiar to Saratoga, or Newport, or Bar Harbor, as the case may be, are as good-natured as they are clever. The satire, when there is any, is of the mildest, and the general tone is that of one glad to look on the brightest side of the cheerful, pleasure-seeking world with which he mingles.—*Christian Union*, N. Y.

PUBLISHED BY HARPER & BROTHERS, NEW YORK.

☞ *Any of the above works sent by mail, postage prepaid, to any part of the United States, Canada, or Mexico, on receipt of the price.*

www.ingramcontent.com/pod-product-compliance
Lightning Source LLC
Chambersburg PA
CBHW021724110726
47902CB00005B/1327